Mothership

GW00697225

By Martin Duffy

ARAN PUBLISHING GROUP LTD.

MOTHERSHIP
First broadcast on RTE Radio in October 1992

First published 1992 by
ARAN PUBLISHING GROUP LTD
46, Charnwood, Bray, Co. Wicklow

Printed in Ireland by Colour Books Ltd
Baldoyle, Co. Dublin. Telephone (01) 325812

Cover design and illustration by
Peter Haigh

Cover typeset by Waugh Print & Design
3/4 Anglesea Lane, Dun Laoghaire, Co. Dublin

Data transfer and book design by STF Publishing
Celbridge. Telephone (01) 627 3378

ISBN 1-897751-00-1

In the twenty-second century twelve young people travel on a dangerous odyssey through the galaxies — but only one young girl, Han, knows the secret at the heart of Mothership.

A fantastic adventure — impossible to put down.

The Author

Martin Duffy has established a strong reputation as a writer, editor and director for television, radio and film. This is his second novel for children and he is working on the sequel.

Martin lives in Monkstown, Co. Dublin.

"Sometimes we'd have the whole river all to ourselves for the longest time. Yonder was the banks and the islands, across the water; and maybe a spark — which was a candle in a cabin window — and sometimes on the water you could see a spark or two — on a raft or a scow, you know; and maybe you could hear a fiddle or a song coming over from one of them crafts. It's lovely to live on a raft."

**The Adventures of Huckleberry Finn,
Mark Twain**

This book is dedicated to my son

Bernard

Safe journey

Mothership

CONTENTS

CHAPTER 1

Storytellers

THE wind howled around her and the chill had numbed her hands. Each blow echoed along the metal shaft but only the slightest dent was made. If only she could break through this welded hatch. She was sure that their lives depended on finding out what lay beyond.

"Jones!," she cried out, as if her frustration and rage could somehow reach him. He had built walls everywhere to stop them from ever finding the truth. "Jones! I hate you!"

Han clutched the metal rim and rested back. The chill of the air mixing with her sweat made her feverish. She had struggled to beat back the hatch knowing that one false move could send her tumbling down into the blades of the fan she could hear swirling far below in the darkness.

"Jones!" Han wanted to cry, although of course she never would. "I'll find a way. And when I do, I know it'll prove that you lied to us."

But for now there was no more she could do. She strapped the sound gun firmly across her shoulder and gripped the rails. Resigned to defeat this time, she made her way back up the shaft to return to the simple world of the living deck. The others thought that was their whole world — that it was all of Mothership. She would bathe away the sweat and grime and sit among them as if she were just like them; as if the fact that they were all the same age meant they were equally innocent. But all the while she'd know, as she had known for many months, that there was more to Mothership than they could imagine. This journey was not what they thought.

* * * *

"Tell the story. Tell the story." They gathered eagerly around Gus. Sometimes they grew bored with the films on the TV wall, the computer games, and the running around. Especially at time for bed when their bodies might be tired but their minds were still awake and thinking too much to keep quiet.

"Come on Gus. Tell it!"

"But you all know it. Someone else can tell it," he protested.

"No one tells it the way you do!"

"You remember what Jones said the best!"

Eve and Anne pleaded with him. Dan was smiling quietly — once he said the word then Gus would relent. Everyone loved the way Gus told the story. Even Han, who would sit back from the rest and keep her knowledge secret, would listen in fascination to the way he told the story.

"Please, Gus, please!"

"Gus will tell the story when you all shut up," Dan said. The others obediently went quiet.

"Okay. Okay I'll tell it," Gus said. He always pretended at first that he was in no mood to tell the story. That way the boys and girls had to encourage him, so they got each other even more excited about hearing him.

Jim and Eve sat together on the floor, arms around each other. At the centre of the rows and rows of seats in the vast, bright, play area of Mothership the six boys and six girls gathered and were still. The shining sphere of the UWPA crest gleamed above them. The computer game screens were blank and no music played. The TV wall shimmered in grey silence. They forgot all these distractions when Gus began:

"Once upon a time a long time ago there were twelve space travellers — two members of each race on Earth — who went on a great adventure across the universe. They travelled to new planets and made friends there and learned things and gathered all kinds of knowledge and wealth. I don't remember Jones ever telling me about any particular adventures, but I have reason to believe that my own father was a doctor who once saved the life of a ruler on a far away planet. As a reward he was offered half the ruler's wealth. My father just accepted a small gift of the biggest and rarest jewel in the universe to bring back to Mothership. The stories of the great adventures are stored on the files of the ship computer — but we can't read them because we have to be sure they don't get damaged or lost. It's the same with the treasures. As the heroes travelled they stored all their discoveries and treasures on Mothership in the part of the ship that's out of bounds. As the adventurers visited the eleven main galaxy kingdoms, one space traveller stayed on each capital planet as an ambassador from Earth."

He paused to enjoy the enthralled looks on their faces.

"The universe is bigger than we can imagine and the journey back with Mothership fully loaded is very slow. Our parents are the heroes of a great adventure, but they will never personally be praised on Earth for their great deeds. Their way of returning to the home planet is through us, their children. Jones was the one chosen to stay with us when we were very small. He left us years ago so that he could travel ahead to Earth on a small and very fast spaceship. He's on Earth now, making all the plans for our big welcoming party."

This was the part of the story they were waiting for. Gus would always act out parts of the story around this point.

"How big will the party be?" Kay asked. Con giggled. It was a ritual. It was like music. They knew the answers to the questions — they'd heard the story countless times — but their words made them part of the storytelling. Gus grinned as he looked around the faces. Fay blushed and glanced at Luke who, as usual, was studying Gus the way he seemed to study everyone he looked at.

"Jones said that it would be the biggest party ever in the history of Earth," Gus said, and some of the boys and girls nodded to each other. "They'll have a big party here first while they study the treasures and discoveries — that's the reason for all the seats and all the bunks and all the room on Mothership. And when we eat..." Some of them laughed. This was Dan's favourite part. He leaned forward in his seat and his belly rested on his lap. His mouth watered at the thought of food and a rumble gurgled in his stomach. "When we eat it won't be the chemical food. No more of that chemical food. No — it'll be the real food like we see in the films. Fresh ice cream — any flavour — and real chocolate, and strawberries, and popcorn, and cakes. You name it. That's what Jones said: 'you name it'. All we want, and whenever we want it. We won't ever have to eat the old food again."

"Never have to eat the old food," Ike repeated. He absolutely hated the food that came out of the machines in the feeding area. The pastes and lumps and thick liquids sometimes made him feel so sick he'd throw up. His one great dream was to eat real food on Earth.

Ben closed his eyes and pictured his own dream. It was a very different one from Ike's. As Ben imagined it, he could almost feel the sun on his face and the lurching of his body with the flow of the river.

"We're going to have sunshine, and live in real homes, and we'll be famous, and we'll meet all the leaders of the six nations. They'll even make films about us — just like the ones we watch here — and Jones said we'd probably have a statue made of each and every one of us."

"When will it happen?" Fay asked.

"Jones said we'd know. He said a message would come. He said we have to be patient."

"It'll happen when it happens," Dan said. He didn't like to hear them talk about how long the journey might be. Even though they were all the same age Dan was the biggest. He was also a bully and so tried to keep the kind of control on them he believed Jones would want.

Gus talked on, telling of parties and honours to come on Earth, and they all felt happier. Sometimes they wondered impatiently if there would ever be an end to their days on Mothership, but as long as they felt everything was going to be all right they would relax again. It might be weeks before their mood needed the reassurance of the story. But Gus would be there to tell it, and it reminded them that at least, even if the journey was long, at the end there would be this excitement and reward.

The story had kept them going through the tedious years of each day being the same as the day before. Their lives consisted of Dan's rule, the same old films to watch, the boring classes that no one bothered with anymore, and the panic they sometimes felt when they realised their world was so small compared to the endless expanse of space they could see outside the portholes.

"When we get home to Planet Earth," Gus continued quietly, "everyone will admire us for living on Mothership. Everyone will praise the way we took care of Mothership and brought back all the treasures. We are very special and we should all be very proud. There's a wonderful time ahead for all of us. Jones said it. Jones said we're going to live happily ever after. All we have to do is wait for the sign."

"Time for bed. Time for bed." Jones voice came from speakers around the room. Their days were measured out through the instructions he had programmed before leaving. The speakers announced time for bed, time to rise, time for food and time for school. They obeyed almost all the time — the only voice instruction they now ignored was time for school because Dan didn't bother with school. Seeing himself as the leader Dan would bully anyone who didn't obey the voice.

"Time for bed," Dan repeated, breaking the silence of their dreams as the story ended. No one objected. They would each go off to lie in their bunks with much to dream of and much to savour. Quietly they left and made their way to the sleeping quarters. They would sleep and maybe dream of Earth while Mothership carried them on through deepest space. Even Fay, who had been waking from strange nightmares about ghosts haunting Mothership and whispering to her, believed she would sleep well.

Han, exhausted by her efforts in the shaft, was only too happy to let sleep free her from the fears and challenges her discoveries had unleashed.

CHAPTER 2

Han and Ben

LUKE was watching the man with the scrunched-up face who talked about the history of superconductivity. The man had a peculiar way of bringing his eyebrows together as he stared from the TV wall. Luke tried to copy it.

"The temperature breakthrough which led to the commercial and domestic use of superconductivity was achieved in 2032 by Doctors Briers and Watts." Luke mimed the words — even though he had no idea what they meant. "They won a Nobel Prize for the discovery, Briers winning her second Nobel Prize twenty years later."

It wasn't that Luke enjoyed attending the classes. He just used them as a way of avoiding Dan. He didn't mind being on his own either. He had the luxury of fifty seats to choose from in any of the four classrooms, and he could spend his time learning to mimic the teachers. Luke was especially good at doing the English Literature teacher — she was the oddest of all.

Sometimes Dan would ask him: "what did you learn in school today, fool?" and if Luke did a funny impersonation he'd get away without being pushed around or ordered out of the play area before time for bed. Because he was the smallest boy, being funny saved him from the worst of Dan's bullying, but finding ways of being funny was a constant effort. Otherwise, he was safe near Dan only when Ben was around — Ben was nearly as big as Dan. He was different too. Long ago he had told Luke he didn't like him trying to be funny all the time and Luke had learned to be quieter around him. He didn't have to obey Ben, or be amusing, or even a good talker to pass the time with him. However, Mothership was a constant danger zone for Luke without Ben.

Secretly he wanted to kill Dan. He never heard any of the others admit to feeling the same way so he kept his ideas to himself. In his portable schoolwork computer, filed under a secret code word, Luke had stored ideas about ways of killing him and cutting up his body and hiding it on Mothership.

As no one was around — everyone else was up in the play area — Luke lifted back the lid of his computer and switched it on. The pale green screen lit up and Luke took one more look around the empty classroom before he typed in his secret code word for the file about Dan. The letters P-I-G-G-I-E opened a file which listed entries about hating Dan and killing him and what kind of fool he was. Luke was reading through them, chuckling very quietly to himself, when he heard a noise from the corridor outside.

In a great panic, he hit the wrong buttons to exit the programme, flicked it shut, and then sat on the little computer to muffle its bleeps of protest as he prayed that Dan wasn't coming to check on him.

He need not have worried. Eve and Jim ran along the corridor past the classrooms playing chase. They ran up the broad spiral and into the play area, giggling loudly. Eve bumped into Con playing table tennis with Kay and knocked her out of the line of a crucial volley. Everyone yelled at them to go away but the two were hardly even aware of anyone else. They ran through the play area and on up the spiral past the feeding area and upwards into the sleeping quarters.

As they ran past the rows of bunks Jim caught Eve and the two landed on a bed. Jim tickled and squeezed Eve and she struggled with him without really wanting him to stop. They seemed to want to spend more and more time with each other and had almost completely given up spending time with anyone else. The two giggled loudly as they rolled on the bed.

"No one's allowed in the sleeping quarters until time for bed." The voice was loud and sharp and neither of them had to think twice before recognising it. Dan stood at the door of his bedroom. They halted and stared at him. Eve hated the way Dan made everyone obey the very rules he ignored. She also hated the way he used Jones' bedroom with the big bed and the TV and music when everyone else had to sleep in bunks.

"You're in the sleeping quarters," she said and Jim stared at her shocked by her defiance.

"I'm different." Dan swaggered past the frame of the bedroom door towards them.

"No you're not. Tell him, Jim."

Jim stood and looked up at Dan. Dan knew he wouldn't be challenged and he grinned.

"Yes," he said, "tell me Jim." He approached the pair, knowing full well that Jim was no match for him. "There's a punishment for anyone who comes into the sleeping quarters before time for bed. The punishment is..."

He stopped. He could see Ben across the room leaning up on his bunk, his calm grey eyes peering down on the scene. The two stared at each other and a tired sigh came from Ben as he put down his favourite book — 'The Adventures of Huckleberry Finn'.

"What's the punishment?" Ben asked quietly.

It had been a long time since Ben and Dan had fought. Ben had won then, and even though Dan had become a lot heavier since and a little taller, he never dared to take on the challenge again. Certainly, he would not take on Ben alone, without Gus or Ike around to back him up. But there was no need for a fight because Ben was no threat to Dan's power. Ben did not care about things like being obeyed, and he was not interested in leading. As long as the two avoided each other there was no need for a showdown.

"We're going now," Jim said, relieved that Dan was distracted from another bullying show of strength. He took Eve by the hand and led her away. Dan and Ben stared at each other. It was plain that neither was going to yield. Finally Dan shrugged his shoulders.

"Stupid running around," he grumbled. "Stupid kids."

Dan went back into his bedroom to flop on the bed and watch one of the old films on disc. Ben went back to reading his book. Both knew a time had to come when Dan would either fight Ben to lay claim to full control of Mothership or else become less daring about his authority.

Ben was not the only rebel beyond Dan's control. Han, with her sound gun, was a far greater threat and was certainly impossible to overpower.

* * * *

At mealtime nearly everyone sat at the one table with Dan at its head — even though there were rows and rows of tables. Luke sat alone at the table nearest the door — just as Dan had ordered a long time before. Not that Luke minded. He just ate his food and stared out a porthole at the stars.

When Ben came in he went to the dispenser and punched in his choice of food. After a moment the tray emerged with hot, coloured chemical proteins.

Ben joined Luke, as usual.

"Hello Ben." Luke considered him a great friend, even though Ben didn't talk much and never seemed to show that he liked anyone. "Would you like to play Tornado Fighters with me later?" Luke's only chance of getting to play the games was if Ben played with him.

"Maybe," Ben replied. They ate quietly. At the main table Dan was talking loudly as he gobbled up more food than anyone else could eat. Dan never seemed to talk about anything, yet he did so louder than anyone else on Mothership and, if he thought someone wasn't paying attention to him, he would taunt and bully until he or she was in desperate tears of fear.

Then Han came in. Han was a strange one. Sometimes she would show up for meals, but recently she was mostly missing all day. No one knew where she spent her time — no one particularly cared. But her boiler suit was streaked with grease and, as usual, she had her sound gun strapped over her shoulder. She looked around at the others with contempt as she went to the food dispenser. Dan watched her and all fell silent, sensing trouble.

"You should be here on time for food," Dan growled, but she ignored him. He threw a food-spattered plastic plate across at her. "Did you hear me?"

Han turned to him and stared. Her smooth, pale brown face showed no sign of reaction. Her dark brown eyes gazed calmly.

"What's up Dan?" her voice was even and strong, "you want another flying lesson?"

Luke almost laughed — but he knew better. Dan would've taken out all his anger for Han on him.

No one knew where she had found the sound gun, but it separated her from the others. Months before, when Han suddenly appeared with the gun, Dan tried to take it and she fired at him. The impact sent him flying across the room. Dan swore afterwards that one day he'd get that gun

— then no one would dare challenge him and he'd be the absolute ruler of Mothership.

"You're going out of bounds, aren't you?," he fumed, "Jones said none of us was ever to go out of bounds."

"Jones is gone," Han said "and I do what I like." She took her food and went to sit alone at a table. Ben watched her though his face showed no hint of his fascination.

"What do you think of Han?" Luke asked.

"She's okay," Ben grunted.

"I like Han."

If Ben were to admit his own feelings, he probably would have agreed.

* * * *

During sleeptime Ben woke up. The light from the corridor sprayed shadows around the wide room. He looked at the bunk where Han should have been sleeping but it was empty. He climbed down — Luke was asleep beneath him and stirred awake as Ben slipped to the floor. Luke stared at him and Ben put a finger to his mouth. Luke nodded, feeling confident of Ben's protection even if he wasn't nearby, and then closed his eyes. Ben quietly made his way out of the sleeping quarters and down the spiral to the play area.

Halting in the corridor, he peeped around the corner and saw Han at one of the computers typing furiously on the keyboard. Ben had almost forgotten that the computers were for anything other than games. Han was busy punching in codes and requests.

Ben saw the words "Mission Flight Plan — Access Denied" come up on the screen. Han shook her head and tried more numbers and more words. Han knew things about Mothership. Eventually he drew away from the door and went back to the sleeping quarters. Han was up to something and Ben wanted to know what it was. He decided to keep a closer watch on her.

"Time to rise. Time to rise." Jones' recorded voice woke them, but they did not get up if Dan slept past the call. Ben woke sharply and saw that Han was already missing — if she had been back to bed at all that night.

Ben carried on with the waking routine. He washed in the long white-tiled bathing area and then collected his vitamin drink and strawberry-flavoured protein snack from the dispenser in the feeding area. He sat quietly with Luke as the others chattered away and Dan's voice boomed over them all.

The day followed the usual dull pattern and there was no sign of Han. She came into the play area once and hung around, watching the activities. She seemed to be waiting for a chance to use one of the computers, but left after a while.

Ben followed her around the curving corridor as she headed for the sleeping quarters. He hoped to find out where she'd spent her time. As if she could sense him, she stopped.

"What do you want?", she asked without even turning.

Ben didn't know what to say at first. No one ever knew how to approach Han and, of course, she could always rely on her sound gun if she felt the need.

"I want to know about Mothership," he finally replied. "You know things and... and I want to know them too."

Han turned and sneered at him. Even if Ben wasn't the worst of them, she reckoned he was no match for her intelligence. She looked at his open, wide-eyed face and felt that at least he was no real threat. Unlike Dan, Ben would never try to force information out of her.

"If you try following me, you'll get a taste of this," she said, patting the gun.

"If I can prove you're going out of bounds I'll tell Dan."

Han smiled — Ben was certainly a hopeless liar.

"You hate Dan as much as I do."

Ben couldn't argue with that. But he didn't want to give up. He wanted to understand.

"Look, I'm just asking you to tell me what you know," he said.

"Anything I know I figured out for myself. The answers are all here. It's just that nobody else ever uses their brains." She walked away. "And if you're following me, you might as well know I'm just going to the toilet."

Ben gave up — he had revealed his curiosity without discovering anything new about Han. So much for quietly keeping an eye on her. He leaned his head against a porthole and gazed out at the stars. This was their life — waking, eating, sleeping. Each day spent in what they'd always called the play area because that's what Jones called it.

Jones shaped their lives. Even in the years since he had left, his rule had held and his voice gave the commands. Jones said that one day there would be a message that would signal the end of their journey. They would arrive on Planet Earth and be able to live like the people in the films. They would live in houses, walk on streets, sit on beaches and play in parks. It was too much to think about sometimes — too much to wait for. It was the stuff of their dreams and hopes and stories. But it was all they had in their monotonous lives.

Ben had found his own private escape from it all a few years before. Jones used to keep books in his room, and Ben was one of the few interested in learning to read. When Jones lived with them Ben had never gone near his special books — the leather bound ones with gold writing on the covers. After Jones left, however, Ben looked through them and came across 'The Adventures of Huckleberry Finn'. As he opened the leaves of that book Ben had been drawn into a world he felt he had been born to live in. Huck Finn quickly became more than Ben's hero — he became another part of Ben, a true person who really lived just like the book said.

Ben liked Huck because neither of them really had a father or mother and both of them liked to keep to themselves and do things their own way. Ben's dream was to go on a raft one day like Huck Finn. Ben wanted to know what it was like to smoke a clay pipe or chew on a straw, or feel the water lapping against his hand. One day he would have the chance to enjoy that kind of independence and freedom. The prison of Mothership would be left behind him — indeed, once the journey was over, Ben doubted that he would ever even sleep under a roof again. He wanted to have as much wild freedom as Huck Finn — and no longer just in his imagination as he read the book over and over again. A real adventure is what Ben craved. It would happen — it had to happen.

He stood there a long while, lost in dreaming his dreams, before realising that Han hadn't come back. She had lied to him.

CHAPTER 3

The First Lie

THERE was no sign of Han in the sleeping quarters and she had not passed him. Ben went up the spiral to the next level, to the store rooms and service areas. She was not there either and Ben found himself standing at the end door.

Jones had told them this was the door to outer space — if they ever tried to open it they'd fall into nothing and go on falling. Ben shuddered as he stared at the door. There was an access keypad beside it with numbers. Nobody ever dared touch this since the time Eve stupidly put her hand on it and got an electric shock so strong it threw her backwards. It was madness to interfere with it anyway.

Ben was shaken from his thoughts when he heard a quiet whirring noise. He looked up to see the camera above the door shift to stare down at him. Jones had said that the cameras around the ship were Mothership's way of watching them.

"It's okay. I'm not doing anything," Ben said to Mothership. But then he thought about it and the word just came out. "Han."

He pressed his ear against the door but heard nothing from the other side. He noticed at this angle, however, that the access keypad had been touched. There were tiny bits of grease on some of the numbers, as if someone with dirty fingers had pressed them. It didn't make sense, yet he was sure that Han was on the other side of that door. He stood to the side of the door — as far away as he could get in case it opened and space tried to reach in and swallow him — and braced himself for an electric shock as he pressed a number that was grease marked.

Nothing happened.

He tried all the marked numbers and still nothing happened. He tried the numbers in a different order, thinking all the while about Jones' warnings. Finally he decided he was being foolish. It was absurd to think that Han was on the other side of the door. She couldn't possibly be — there was nothing there but space and the stars. Ben was about to walk away when the door panels drew back.

It wasn't outer space. It was a tiny bright room. Ben stared at it for a while. It was so small no more than six people could stand inside. Ben knew he couldn't walk away from this chance for adventure, yet he needed all his courage to take a step in.

"Hello?" he called, and realised it was stupid to expect a reply. The room didn't seem to lead anywhere or to have another exit. What was its function? Was it a trap of some kind? The panels began to close, and at the last moment Ben tried to jump out. Before he could, the panels slid shut with a soft, firm, thud.

Ben punched at the walls. They were solid and there was no way out.

"Hello?" he called again.

He heard a noise and looked up. The ceiling was opening and the floor was starting to rise. Ben cried out. Above him he could see a long bright circular tunnel with rails and grips set in the curved walls. Impossible! As the rising floor lifted him further into the tunnel his feet left the ground. Ben was floating!

He screamed in panic as he was gently launched into the tunnel. He tried to grab the ceiling of the small chamber — but the ceiling panels were closing and his fingers could be chopped off. He let go and drifted helplessly up into the tunnel, trying to reach for the grips but not floating close enough to them. Reaching this way and that, he started rolling in mid air.

"Help! Help me!"

He imagined himself being trapped there forever. He knew that none of the others would ever come through the door. This was his punishment for disobeying Jones and he could see no escape.

"Help me!"

Dizzy now, he glimpsed a door opening at the far end of the tunnel. A figure emerged. It was Han. She looked down at him and smiled.

"Help me!" he pleaded, "I... I'm going to be sick!"

She came towards him by expertly gripping the rails with her feet.

"Calm down and I'll grab you," she called, and Ben stopped all movement. She reached him and spun his weightless body around. She sniggered as she looked at his terrified face.

"Idiot. Grab the rails with your feet and follow me," she said. Ben was too scared to do anything but thank her. He felt Han was familiar with this bizarre experience and enjoyed feeling superior to him.

They went head first into the chamber at the far end of the tunnel. Han made him hold the rails as the floor closed beneath them.

"There's no gravity in the links between the decks," she said.

"Gravity?"

"What keeps us on the ground. Weight. This." As Han spoke, a very familiar sensation returned. He had no interest in physics at school and only became aware of weight and gravity when they disappeared.

"Are you still sure you want to follow me?" Han asked. Ben wasn't sure anymore, but he would not admit this to Han.

"I want to know what you know." Ben was just beginning to recover from the experience of weightlessness when the chamber panels opened.

"Then your education begins. This is control deck," Han announced as she stepped out of the chamber. Ben didn't move. Han looked back at him, seeing the fear in his eyes. "Look — you know how the link works now. The access code for this deck is 5613. To go back it's 4613. If you want I'll punch in the code and you can go back right now."

"No. No," he said, but still didn't move. Han shook her head in annoyance.

"Well come on out."

Ben summoned up his courage, let go of the rail, and followed Han into a round corridor much like the one down at the end of the classroom level. Han smiled slightly as she watched Ben stare wide-eyed around him.

"There's more than we know," she said. "Much more than Jones told us — more than you can imagine."

The winding corridor led past rooms in which computers purred. Everything was bright, clean and still. Ben had never experienced such silence. Mothership for him was a place which echoed with the noise of arguing voices and booming music or TV. The silence frightened him — it was as if he had stepped into a tomb — and only the need to keep a brave face in front of Han stopped him from running away.

"I first made my way to this deck months ago", she explained, "when I figured out how to use the access keypad. Ever since then I've been studying it and how Mothership works."

The two came out to a high, open area in which stood a tall silver dome. Gleaming pipes sprayed out from the dome and were connected to networks of pipes around the walls. To Ben, the metal structure seemed like a statue to some god of science. He had never seen anything like it in the video discs or the classes.

"This is the cold fusion reactor," Han said in a very matter-of-fact tone, "it powers Mothership. It has the capacity to carry us for three hundred years — what does that tell you?"

Ben had no answer. He stood at the rail around the reactor.

"It's now only on one tenth power — almost shut down," Han continued. Again, Ben did not understand enough to make any response. Han despaired of him.

"Come on," she said. Han walked to another small chamber — this one was all glass and led upwards through a glass tube. Ben stepped reluctantly inside, this time grabbing hold of the rails very firmly.

"You won't lose gravity in an ordinary elevator, you dumbwit," Han said.

The glass panel closed and they rose up. Ben watched in amazement as they passed above the dome and then into a chamber like the one at the link. When the door opened again they were facing a semi-circular console in a room lined with screens, controls, and computers.

Lights flashed and the computers very quietly bleeped in harmony as if the place were alive. Ben thought that perhaps there were ghosts at the controls, or that someone had just stepped away and was about to return and catch both of them. Han stepped confidently into the room, but Ben didn't move until the door began to close on him.

"This is master control," Han said with a sweep of her

arm. "This is where everything on Mothership is monitored, recorded, decided, and executed. If we weren't on remote control, this is where the flight crew would be operating from."

It was more than Ben could believe. To him, the world of Mothership had been a definite place — the living quarters and the stores — powered by rockets they couldn't see. This place wasn't like anything Jones had led them to believe existed. Han sat in one of the chairs and expertly keyed in an instruction.

"Don't touch anything!" Ben cried, but she just grinned as she carried on.

"I can remember from when we were small that Jones wasn't with us all the time," she said, "he'd be missing for ages. When he'd come back if anyone asked where he'd been he used to make up some story of being around or watching us or something. Well, this is where he was. Jones did a lot of work here."

As Han keyed in her request a three-dimensional shape formed clear and startling. Ben moved forward. It showed a gigantic ship of five decks, each deck having special functions — control, living, life support, cargo, and transport. They were now on control deck — the smallest of the five sections, even though it contained the control room, reactor and the computer rooms they had passed.

The world that Ben had thought of as being everything was just one part of a vast ship making its way through space. The group were like tiny specks on this huge, majestic ship. Han could see the shock on his face.

"This is it," she said, "this is where we are. Mothership. Judging by what I've studied, I'd say it's probably the biggest spaceship ever made. It's beautiful, isn't it?"

Ben reached out to touch the screen as if that might wake him up or convince him that this was all some trick — a spell Han was weaving on him.

"We shouldn't be here," he mumbled.

"We have a right to know where we are and where we're going and why we're here. Listening to Gus tell tales handed down from Jones isn't enough. Not for me. Is it enough for you?" she asked.

Ben's mind was racing — caught up in a fierce argument. On the one hand he felt they had no right to be in this part of Mothership — yet on the other hand he knew the deep secret that was being unlocked would change his view of truth.

"I don't understand why no one else asks questions," Han said. "Maybe it's because I'm the only one who kept on going to classes. Or maybe it's because I'm the only one who didn't trust Jones."

Ben wasn't listening to Han. For the first time ever he was asking himself the most obvious question of all and Jones' answer no longer held any truth.

"Do you know it?" he asked. "Do you know where we are?" Han punched in more instructions and a chart came up on the screen. It showed a flight path with Earth at one end and a planet further into the galaxy at the other end.

Ben touched the line traced across screen. He looked at Han, the green light of the screen across their faces — "Is that where I am?"

"A lot of information can't be accessed," Han replied. "That's the flight path we're on, but I don't know where we are on the journey. We could be approaching Earth or not even half way."

"Han — we shouldn't be out of bounds interfering with all this. It's dangerous."

"I don't know the whole answer," Han wasn't the kind of person to accept the old rules, "but there are things I do know. Firstly, there's something about our being born that wasn't part of the original plan, and secondly, there's something wrong with Mothership."

Han keyed in another request and the screen came to life with a new image. The heading was 'ship status', and it showed the outline of the decks. Both the life support and the cargo decks showed flashing red lights in sections. She then focused in on a damage section and requested more detail. The screen flashed the words 'Access Denied'.

"Jones has the controls set up so that I can't find out what effect the damage is having on the flight, or what our chances of survival are, or if the damage can be repaired."

Ben looked at the damage report.

"Jones said everything was fine. He's waiting for us on Earth."

"Jones was a liar," Han said. "He bailed out because he knew the whole truth."

She studied Ben's face for his reaction, wondering just how much she could trust him.

"I've never been able to figure out what goes on in your head," she said, "but I don't want to spend the rest of my life drifting through space and I imagine you might feel the same way. I reckon the only way to find out exactly what's going on is to get to the damaged decks, and I've been trying to do that for a long time. But Jones has blocked the way by disconnecting the access keypad for the link at the bottom of our living deck down to the life support deck. He's also built barriers that I'm not strong enough to break through by myself. I need some extra muscle power to help me reach the rest of Mothership."

Ben's first thought was that it was forbidden to go out of bounds — an adult had said so. But then, Ben reasoned, there was undeniably something wrong with Mothership — could he ignore that fact? Of course not. Once the first lie had been revealed, more questions had to be asked.

For the first time in his life, Ben saw a chance of living a real adventure — not just reading one. Certainly he didn't want to find out that they were stranded on a ship going nowhere. But the idea of setting out on a journey of discovery which would lead to the whole truth about Mothership was irresistible.

He thought about Huckleberry Finn and couldn't imagine his hero feeling afraid. Ben resolved not to let fear get in the way of exposing these lies.

"You can count me in," he said.

"You know we can't tell anyone else."

"I know for sure," Ben said, "if Dan ever found out what we're doing he'd go crazy."

CHAPTER 4

Life Support

T HEY returned separately to the living deck to avoid the impression of having been away together. Their plan was to set off as soon as possible after time for bed so that Han could show Ben the route she'd been trying to make into the life support deck.

Ben had lately been spending a lot of his time away from the others. Staying in the play area with them, in the light of his new discoveries, only made him feel all the more separate from them. The way of life they had developed since Jones had left now seemed so strange.

Ben tried to remember what it had been like when Jones was around. It was so long ago that he could only remember vague things, like the fact that Jones never allowed any misbehaviour, and he hadn't seemed to like any of them. Ben remembered also that there had been some kind of order which had faded with time. They didn't wash themselves or change their clothes as regularly as they were supposed to, and the computer schoolbooks they each owned were little used even though Jones had said they could store and teach anything.

Thinking back, Ben could barely remember the day Jones left. Jones had been very quick about announcing his departure, and his parting speech had been very simple. There was no room for doubt in his promises — Jones assured them all that Earth was close and a sign would soon come. Jones said he would travel ahead to Earth to speed up the preparations for their arrival. But how long ago had that been?

Ben's memories of fearing Jones were so dim. Jones had always punished them if they cried. After he left no one admitted just how frightened they were even though the loss of an adult had frightened them greatly.

Ben felt older than he wanted to feel and different from the others. He wanted to tell them all that things on Mothership were not as they thought or pretended to remember. But he forced himself to stay quiet.

After mealtime Ben played a computer game with Luke, mostly to keep his mind off his fear and excitement. Fay and Anne had another argument — they were always arguing — but at least this time Dan did not get involved. He was too busy loudly saying the lines from his favourite cartoon video disc which he insisted on watching on the main screen in the play area. Eventually, Ben went to bed early to get some rest before the work ahead. He didn't expect to sleep, but as his mind swam in the pool of new discoveries sleep came.

Ben had a familiar dream. In it he was very young - little more than a baby — and he was lying on soft white foam. Suddenly above him there was the face of a woman. She was smiling down at him saying "Mommy, Mommy", and he smiled back at her, feeling impossibly small. She lifted him up and felt warm and soft. The sense of being cradled by her made him feel overjoyed.

Something told him in the dream that this is what it means to be a child. You can trust and be happy. Everything is safe, and the world is certain.

But then in the dream Ben started to grow bigger and the comfort of the cradle shrank from him. The warmth faded as he became himself and looked around for Mommy. She was gone and he was alone as the light around him faded. There was nothing to protect him anymore and there was no certainty. He had to find his own way with only himself to trust in the darkness.

Ben awoke sharply. Everyone was asleep.

He crept silently to Han's bunk and touched her shoulder. She instinctively grabbed her gun, but then recognised Ben. They slipped out of the sleeping quarters and down the spiral corridor to the bottom level beyond the classrooms. Neither of them had noticed Luke waking up and watching them leave.

*   *   *   *

"This won't be easy," Han said, "I reckon life support deck is where we get our air, food and water from. This is the main pipe feeding air into our deck. The maintenance hatch here will take us into the pipe so we climb down parallel to the sealed link and into the next deck. There's a maintenance hatch to that deck too — but Jones has welded it shut. If we can get it open we'll be through to life support deck."

"You've already been inside the pipe?" Ben asked.

"It's tough going," Han said, "though maybe it won't be so bad for you since you're bigger than me."

Ben felt afraid but also exhilarated.

"Let's do it," he said.

"You won't like this one bit," Han warned. She switched on her torch and closed the wall panel on the corridor behind them. Together they lifted back the hatch on the big pipe.

Even though Ben had seen the layout of Motherhip and knew three decks lay beneath, Jones' voice in his head kept warning him that they were heading towards the flames of the ship rockets.

"Gravity is the same way for each deck. We're heading into the top floor of the next deck, so we have to go feet first. Ready?"

Ben nodded and Han crawled first into the pipe. A cold sharp wind blew at them as they clambered down the tiny rungs inside. Their steps echoed through the pipe which extended above and below for what seemed like eternity. The rungs were bitterly cold to the touch, and as the light from Han's torch flickered around the pipe Ben tried not to think about how far he'd fall if his numbing hands were to lose their grip.

When they reached the link area, Ben found himself drifting when he tried to rest his foot on the rungs beneath.

"You have to use your own body now," Han said. "Push your back against the wall and force yourself along."

Ben hated the sensation. Eventually he could feel gravity again, and they finally reached the maintenance hatch on the other side. There was a lip around its base where they could both stand and hold on to metal rungs.

Ben could see the dents where Han had tried to force the hatch open. He tried to peer through the dense mesh porthole to see what lay beyond but it was impossible.

"Have you tried the sound gun?" Ben was panting.

"Once. It nearly blew my ears out."

"Then maybe we should use it as a hammer."

"That'll break it."

Ben gave the hatch a few kicks. The pipe dented slightly, but the hatch held firm.

"What happens if we go further on?"

"You get closer and closer to the generator. No more

hatches." Maybe it was the eerie light reflecting onto Han's face, but Ben thought he saw a trace of fear. "I haven't gone all the way down."

Ben leaned back against the wall of the pipe and the cold seeped in to chill the sweat on his back. He had no clever ideas and no wish to take any chances of losing his grip.

"Okay", he finally said, "let's see what happens when we just use force together."

They started kicking, and although Ben made deeper dents, their progress was slight. Ben finally signalled a halt and the two breathlessly reviewed their efforts. Ben noticed a slight break in the mesh of the hatch and he realised that with enough force he could kick that back to make a gap for them both to squeeze through.

"Keep well clear of me," he said as he climbed up a few rungs. He gripped a rung very firmly and then swung his body back like a pendulum to crash his feet into the mesh.

"It's too dangerous!" Han cried.

Ben didn't reply — he didn't want to think about the danger. He swung back and crashed again. This time he lost his grip with one hand and for a moment he dangled by the other frozen hand with the growl of the generator far beneath him seeming to grow louder.

"We'll try some other way," Han said desperately. But Ben was stubborn — he knew he was strong enough to break through the mesh. He swung again and this time it gave way a little more. In the end there was enough of a gap to force their way through.

"You did it!" Han said as she climbed up beside him.

"No problem," Ben lied.

When they squeezed through the gap they were confronted by a darkness so vast that the weak torch light didn't reach the walls. It reminded Ben of his dream, and he shuddered. They clambered down the grips on the outside of the pipe and walked away from it.

Looking around in the torch light, Han finally saw a

door. They found that it too was sealed, but Han felt it was safe to use the sound gun. Ben stood beside her as she pulled the trigger. Even though the gun jolted in her grip, nothing seemed to come from the muzzle. Yet the sound wave impact struck so hard that the door immediately buckled. With another blast the door fell away. Light flooded in on their blinded eyes.

They stepped out into a bright round corridor which wound downwards. Han and Ben stood close together, knowing that their only safety was in each other. They said nothing.

There was a foul smell in the air that made them feel sick, and Han reckoned it was caused by a plant to recycle body waste. When they came to a door marked "Maintenance Three", they expected to find the source of the smell. Ben opened the door by pressing a button at the side. When the panels slid back they saw a network of pumps and machines inside, all busily humming away. The air was clean in the room, however. The smell returned onlywhen they stepped back into the corridor. It became stronger as they carried on downwards.

They came to tall, wide bay doors. The sign overhead said "Life Support".

"But we've been through the life support systems," Han said. "Air, water, human waste. So what's this?"

Without thinking, Ben walked to the bay door which automatically drew back. The stench that hit them was so strong that they reeled and covered their faces.

"This must be part of the damage," Han said.

"We won't be able to breathe in there."

"Wait. Wait."

The two knelt down and gasped fitfully, trying not to breathe the foul air. In spite of the revolting smell, Han was far too eager to uncover more of the mystery to turn back now.

"We'll jam the doors open," she said, "come on."

The two stepped through the doors. Already the foulest

air had escaped and the stench was beginning to fade. The doors obviously hadn't been opened in a very long time.

They were on the top balcony of a huge, multi-layered chamber. Silver pipes spread down from the ceiling to banks of grey blocks. Below them were rows and layers of what appeared to be lockers, surrounded by gangways and computer terminals. At the centre of the floor far beneath were six long silver modules. Each module was attached to its own computer and had a slim window at its head.

"What is this?" Ben gasped. He expected Han to understand such things, but she was just as baffled. She stepped forward and gripped the rail as she looked down at the mute technology.

"What have we found?"

CHAPTER 5

Heroes

THEY went to the glass-panelled elevator leading down to ground level, but nothing happened when they pressed the button. Instead, they climbed down an emergency ladder to the nearest row of grey lockers. Ben walked along them while Han stayed at a computer trying entries on the keyboard. Ben stopped at a locker and tinkered with the few buttons and dials on its door.

"These are wombs," Han finally announced.

"What?"

"Wombs. You know what a womb is."

Ben looked at her blankly.

"A womb is what a mammal grows in. It's what a mother has."

Han walked along the row of lockers, touching them.

"These are for cattle." She rushed on to the next block, her voice rising in excitement. "These are for pigs. And these sheep. This is livestock. And domestic animals."

She turned to Ben.

"You see? You see what this means?" Her voice was trembling. She raced down the ladder to the next level as Ben tried to reason out what Han saw so clearly. He looked around at the computers and technology and understood — this whole area was devoted to the storing and breeding of Earth life.

"Who switches them on? Who's to do all this?" he shouted after her, but Han was busy working at another keyboard. "Is this something we're supposed to do?"

He followed her down and was about to join her when he noticed something different about one of the blocks at this level. All twelve lockers were open. As he walked towards them a cold tingle ran down the back of his neck. He began to realise just what this meant.

He reached inside one of the opened lockers and touched a dried plastic-like film around its base. He turned to Han.

"Yes," she said, her eyes pinched and glaring, "we were born here. Six boys, six girls. Racial couples. All the same age. All produced here at the very same time."

"Produced," Ben repeated. It made his birth seem like nothing. It made their lives seem unimportant.

"There are so many of these," he said, looking at the blocks.

"Designed for two hundred humans. Just like the living area — set up for two hundred."

Ben walked towards her. Han tapped at the keyboard and went to a locker. She hit a button and it opened. Inside was a jelly-like substance with small tubes leading to a central point.

"Of course. The eggs aren't stored here. They're planted here and then set to grow." She looked down at the equipment below. "That must be where the fertilised eggs are stored."

"Yes," he said "but that's where the smell is still coming from."

As they went down together Ben felt they were stepping back in time to the lost pieces of a puzzle — evidence of a truth the children on Mothership could never have imagined.

The technology seemed so perfect and powerful, yet plainly something was very wrong. There was a sealed door with thermostats and computer read-outs. Han studied these as Ben went to the six long modules. Each module had a read-out screen. Two of the screens showed the word 'Inactive'. Ben went to the first of these and gripped the handle. The top lifted back to reveal a bed and an array of wires and connections.

The screen over the next module showed only flat lines. Ben tried to open it but it wouldn't budge. Wanting to see inside, he hoisted himself up onto the module and peered through the slim glass window. A white skull stared back at him through slimy eye sockets.

Ben slid off the module and cried out in panic. Han raced to him.

"Dead people inside," he gasped. "a skeleton."

"All the stored life has been killed," Han said. "The door I checked leads to the storage unit for the fertilised eggs. The unit doesn't work anymore. All the eggs, and these adults. Dead. This is where the damage is. Maybe it starts here and goes on down into the next deck."

Ben felt very scared. The more they found out, the less certain he felt about anything. Jones had said that the extra space in the living area was to give them room to play. Jones had said that everything was going fine and they were special.

He never told them about the damage to Mothership or that death was on board with them.

"What's going to happen to us?" he asked. Han looked at him and smiled.

"Even if it's bad it's better to know, isn't it?" She

gripped his arm to reassure him. "We have to find the truth. We have to know exactly what we're dealing with."

All Ben felt was a sense of betrayal. He had lived a lie all this time.

"Are these the heroes?" he demanded. "Are these the ones Jones said were on the planets Mothership had visited? What's going on?"

Han gave a cynical little smile as she looked around. For her, their shrinking world confirmed her worst suspicions. She looked at Ben, wondering if and when he would let go of the old ideas in his head.

"We're cargo," she said, "but I don't understand why — yet. We've got to keep moving on now. We've got to make it to the next deck."

"Cargo?" Ben repeated. The word made him feel so trivial. Gus had told stories of heroes, and though Ben could accept that they weren't heroes he couldn't accept the idea that they were as unremarkable as cattle or pigs.

"It'll be okay," Han said, "we'll understand more if we move on."

"I don't want to," Ben said, "I've seen enough."

"You can't go back now and you know it. We've already seen too much to be able to lie to ourselves the way Jones lied to us. Come on. Let's move."

Han was walking away when Ben called out.

"Han. These people. These dead people. Could they be our parents?"

She thought for a moment.

"We don't know what race they were. But it seems unlikely they were our parents. The twelve of us have more variations of racial types than you can get from six parents. The only sure thing is that there won't be any more of us getting produced."

Han moved on without hesitation and Ben followed. Her confident stride was reassuring. When they arrived at the end door of the deck, Han paused.

"If the damage starts from here we can't be sure what

to expect in the next deck. There might be no air in it. We have to be extremely careful."

On the access keypad she punched in 5613, the same number she had used to get on the control deck . Nothing happened. Then she realised that the number must change with each deck and punched in 2613. The panels of the link door opened.

They knew the small chamber would lead to a tunnel linking with the storage deck. As they stepped in Ben took a deep breath. If this was to be the last of the air he wanted to hold onto it as long as possible and learn as much as he could about the next deck before dying.

They drifted weightless into the bright tunnel. Han smiled at Ben, pretending more confidence than she felt. They caught the grips and made their way along the link to enter the chamber which led into the cargo deck. Once weight had been restored, Han held her gun ready for action.

When the door opened Ben stepped out and looked around. There was nothing to indicate damage. He held up his hand in warning to Han as he inhaled deeply. The air was stale but breathable.

They walked quietly along the corridor, passing doors marked 'Tools' and 'Clothing'. Was this the treasure Mothership was bringing back to Earth from the voyages across the galaxy?

Ben touched the button of a door marked 'Seed Storage' and it opened silently. Inside were rows and racks of containers — all untouched. The same silent, dead, cleanliness was everywhere. It was as though the ship were built to teem with life and industry but instead lay in suspense like the four crew members must have been before they died.

"What does it mean?" Ben whispered.

Han couldn't answer. All the materials they saw originated on Earth.

They carried on along the bright, silent, corridor and

came to an open door marked 'Medical Supplies'. Outside it on the floor lay a small broken jar surrounded by a moist green stain. Han noticed a shoeprint on the stain and measured its size against her own. It was an adult footprint.

CHAPTER 6

Alone

THE medical supplies room contained lines of shelves, some stacked with packets and jars. Other shelves had been completely cleared. Han and Ben walked through a glass door which led into a laboratory.

In the laboratory test tubes and other equipment were strewn around on benches. One bench had been used frequently. Han touched the fine white dust on it.

"Someone's done a lot of work here," she said.

"I don't think we should carry on alone anymore," Ben said, "I don't think it's safe just for the two of us. If anything happened to us here we'd never be found."

"My God you're stupid," Han sighed, "you don't understand yet — do you? We're not alone here. There's someone on this deck."

She gripped her gun, ready for use, and strode out into the corridor. Ben trailed behind feeling that he couldn't leave Han now. He thought of the two empty modules beside the four with the skeletons. If one had been for Jones, was the other for the person now on the cargo deck?

They continued down the winding corridor. The stillness was so total that Ben thought he could hear his heartbeat. At regular intervals other corridors criss-crossed at a central point. Everywhere there were doors, all titled with the different kinds of supplies inside.

Eventually, opened bay doors led onto a catwalk circling the top of a tall chamber. The levels below were stacked with plastic containers. On the ground floor there were huge crates. The main lighting didn't work, and Han and Ben peered down into a darkness illuminated only by some dim strip lights far below.

There was something very different about this place. Something repulsive was in the air. They followed the arch of the catwalk until Han stopped and pointed down. Stacks of books were strewn around the floor near a crate and, ducking down, Han and Ben could see that this crate had been emptied of its contents and was lit inside by a small strip light.

"We have to go back," Ben whispered.

"No way," Han said. She crawled along the metal floor of the catwalk, hoping to get a clearer view inside the hut. Ben was exasperated by the way Han always threw herself into danger. They came to a ladder leading down to the floor and Han looked to Ben.

"I'm going down," she said. "You don't have to come with me."

"What should I do?" he asked, "stay up here and have a rest?"

They made their way silently down the ladder. There was so much shadow and so little light that Ben thought he could sense movement everywhere. When they reached the floor, Han rested her finger on the trigger of the sound gun and prepared to react instantly to any threat. They moved silently along the crates, coming closer to the opened one. There were foul smells, and in the darkness Han kicked a small empty carton which skipped along the floor.

They froze, waiting to hear a noise. Nothing stirred, so they moved on. Soon they were beside the emptied crate, stepping their way through books, boxes, and emptied food tubes. Han rested briefly against the side of the crate before finally peering cautiously around it. She slowly stepped out into the dim light, her gun trained forward. Ben silently joined her.

The floor of the crate was strewn with rubbish and tattered blankets. A TV in one corner was piled high with heaps of video discs. In the other corner was a mattress covered by many old blankets. A dull strip light shone down on a mass of greasy black hair almost hidden by the blankets. There was definitely someone in the bed.

Han and Ben looked at each other. Neither of them could bear the thought of turning back now. They moved forward together, the silence closing in around them as they drew closer to the motionless body under the blankets.

Near the top of the bed were empty laboratory tubes and broken needles which they carefully avoided stepping on.

Ben knelt on one knee beside the mattress and slowly drew the blankets back to reveal a pale white face in a sweaty tangle of beard and hair. Ben gasped and Han aimed the gun directly at the motionless head.

"Is he dead?" Han whispered. Ben looked at her, shrugging his shoulders, then looked back at the man. The man's eyes were open and glaring up at him.

"Aaaagh!" The man roared, revealing blackened teeth in a mouth lost in the beard.

Ben froze in terror. Han grabbed him and pulled him away in the instant the man sprang forward to clutch him with thin, purple hands.

"Aaagh!" The man screamed again and again, waking

from some horrible nightmare or still living it and finding it peopled by these figures. "Aaagh!"

Ben fell over in the dark outside the crate but Han clenched his collar and yanked him to his feet. They slipped and raced through the maze of crates as the man ran after them. He knew his terrain and when for one instant they thought they'd lost him he appeared in front of them. Han and Ben screamed.

"Are you dead?" the man shrieked back. His face was wild. His boiler suit was tattered and sweat-streaked. His black hair coiled like a nest of snakes around his face. "Are you dead?"

Instinctively Han fired a shot which threw the wild man off his feet to crash into a crate behind. They raced desperately away, the wailing of the man spurring them to run faster.

They reached the foot of the ladder and clambered up. Soon the man was nearby, shouting.

"Come back! You!" Ben looked down into the man's wild face. His eyes were red, his skin pale and wet. He looked like a demon. But then with a surge of dread Ben realised that he recognised him. It was Jones.

"You! You! Come here!" Jones yelled. Ben was rooted to the spot, staring down. Jones slowly made his way up. All Ben could think of was that Jones was the adult — the one you always had to obey. Han realised Ben had stopped climbing and roared back at him to move.

"It's Jones! Han, it's Jones!" Ben shouted.

Jones drew closer to Ben, so close Ben could smell his stale breath.

"We have to get away from him!" Han yelled. The man and boy stared at each other. Ben was transfixed.

"Jones," Ben said, helplessly.

Jones pointed a shaking finger.

"You're dead," he wheezed, anger and hatred blazing from his eyes. Terror jarred Ben out of his indecision, and he quickly sprang grip by grip up the ladder until he joined

Han on the catwalk. Beneath them, the frail man climbed the ladder slowly and with great difficulty.

"Maybe he's sick," Ben said, "maybe we should help him."

"Are you crazy?" Han snapped, running on.

"But it's Jones."

"What have you seen so far to make you believe we can trust him?"

Ben raced after her as fast as his feet could carry him. He caught up with Han and they fled in fear past a seemingly endless maze of doors and corridors.

When Han reached the end door, she fumbled and punched in the wrong numbers on the access keypad. The door remained shut.Realising her mistake she punched in the correct numbers and waited desperately. There was no sight or sound of Jones.

At last the panels drew back and the two fell into the chamber. Ben clutched the rails but Han stood with her sound gun at the ready until at last the panels slid shut. Then she gripped the rails and the ceiling opened to reveal the link tunnel above them.

They made their way to the life support chamber as quickly as they could. Near to exhaustion, they fled up the spiral stairs until they reached eventually the first maintenance area and the huge pipe. They crawled through the air shaft into the living area deck.

"What do we do now? What do we do now?" Ben was in a panic.

"He's crazy," Han said "we've got to warn the others. We have to get ready to fight him off. Once he knows that we've found out about him he's bound to come after us."

"Have you got more guns?"

"I found this one in the control deck. There are more up there."

"More? Then why didn't you give me one?"

"I didn't trust you then," she replied, "I trust you now."

"We have to tell the others," Ben said, "stand guard at

the link door while I warn the rest and gather guns. We have to stop Jones."

When they climbed out of the air supply pipe Ben sat breathless on the floor behind the panel and stared at Han. They had unleashed something now — the truth would affect all of them.

"He could do anything," Han said, "he's on the deck that gives us our air, water, and supplies. He could kill us without ever setting foot on this deck."

Ben wearily closed the maintenance hatch.

"Has he been living there all those years? That must be what drove him mad."

"No. More than that," Han's voice was cold and hard, "I'll bet he was crazy before he left us. That's how I remember him. Crazy."

Han lifted the panel into the corridor and looked out — there was no sign of anyone. Ben slipped out quietly, but as he stood up he felt a hand on his shoulder and spun around.

It was Luke.

"Luke — what are you doing here?"

His face was puffed and red, and his eyes were bulging as if they were awash in uncried tears.

"Hiding," he said weakly, "hiding from Dan."

Ben rested a hand on his shoulder.

"What's wrong Luke?"

"Where have you been? Where'd you go?" Luke started sobbing. Han climbed out and the three walked to the nearest classroom.

"It's okay. It's okay," Ben tried to reassure the smaller boy.

"I saw you go," Luke gulped between his sobs, "I didn't know what you were doing. I thought you were dead. I thought you'd fallen into space. And then... then I got a smell through the air vents. I thought you'd got burned in the rockets, I... I thought all kinds of things."

"We went searching," Ben said. "It's okay."

"You didn't tell the others did you?" Han asked.

Luke's soupy eyes glanced at her.

"Yeah I did." Han's heart sank. Luke wiped his tear-stained face as he spoke. "First Dan hit me and said I was lying. Then when no one could find you he went crazy. He said that if you went out this end door you'd be in the rockets and burned up and stopping them from working. When he couldn't figure it out, he tried to open the door on the top level to see if you were there. He got real mad."

Han immediately realised what that could mean. She ran out of the room.

"Han! Han wait'" Ben called. He looked at Luke, who had innocently made their problem worse, then raced after Han. He could guess what Dan had done and how impossible had become their chances of defending themselves against Jones.

CHAPTER 7

Dan

HAN raced up the corridor past Anne and Gus, ignoring their cries to stop. Ben and a breathless Luke followed her. Han halted abruptly when she saw the access keypad beside the end door. Dan had smashed it to pieces. They stared at it in disbelief. Dan came strutting up behind them with some of the others. He sneered as they looked at the damage he had caused.

"Where have you two been?" he demanded. Han turned to him and roared.

"You idiot! You did this! You've wrecked the keypad!"

"It wouldn't work," Dan said smugly, "and besides, no one is allowed out of bounds and you broke the rules."

Instantly Ben attacked him, raging and roaring as he punched into Dan's fat chest. All his own anger and fear exploded as Dan squealed, unable to gain control. Ben was strong and quick, and only Dan's bulky power prevented him from being pinned down. He called out to Gus and Jim to drag Ben off and he rolled away, tumbling into Han as she pulled the gun from her shoulder. Dan dragged her down and flung his dead weight on top of her, seizing the sound gun.

Dan spun around on the floor and fired at Ben — hitting the others at the same time. The fighting bodies were thrown against the wall. As Dan got to his feet Han jumped on him from behind but he flopped back, slamming her against the wall. Luke ran to her aid. Dan fired at him also and Luke flew back through the air.

"Now I have the power," Dan laughed. "Now you all do as I say. No more out of bounds. No more disobeying me. Now I rule Mothership."

"We found Jones," Ben gasped. "He's crazy. He's on his way here. He's going to attack us."

Dan hesitated for a moment. Then he sneered.

"What a dumb liar. You expect us to believe that even for one second?"

"If you hadn't broken the keypad we could've proved it," Han shouted, "you know nothing about Mothership — or the danger we're in. We need more guns to defend ourselves."

"We've seen things," Ben tried to convince the others, "this is just one part of Mothership. There's a control deck up there, and beneath us a whole deck where we were stored like seeds of the human race. That's all been destroyed. There are dead people down there."

Fay stepped forward. She'd never before talked about her strange dreams of ghosts on Mothership, and this was the first indication that there might be something to the dreams.

"Dead?" she asked.

"There's more than we know." Han turned to her. "Jones didn't tell us the truth, and he's still here. You should see what's going on in Mothership. And if Dan hadn't destroyed the access keypad I could've taken you to the control deck where you could've seen for yourselves."

"No more!" Dan shouted. "We know what Jones told us

before he left. And he said we were never to go out of bounds - for our own safety. If you were in the engines of Mothership you better not've broken anything."

"You haven't seen the rest of Mothership," Ben said. "We have. We're in real trouble."

"That's all lies," Dan snapped. "I say none of us believe you."

"You have to believe us," Han insisted, "if we don't do something either Jones will get us or we'll go wandering on in space. Mothership is damaged. We've seen some of the damage."

"Wait - wait," Ben said, "we could get into the control deck by the air supply pipe. Then you'd see. And we'd be able to arm ourselves against Jones."

Dan strutted over to Ben and aimed the gun at him.

"You two can't hide the trouble you're in by saying things about Jones."

"We should give them a chance to prove it," Fay said. "I think that there really is more on this ship than we know about."

"You're just a fool," Dan said, "and Han and Ben are now prisoners. It's the only way to stop them from causing any more damage to Mothership. Tie them up."

*   *   *   *

Jones' hands were shaking as he rooted around in the blankets and on the floor near his bed. He didn't want to leave any supplies behind. He'd stored everything in his little black bag - was there a time, he wondered, when he kept his technical instruments in it? — no. Maybe that Jones no longer existed.

He left his home behind and slung the bag across his shoulder to secure it as he climbed the ladder. Each time he put weight on his left foot pain shot through him like a spear. He had slipped coming down off the ladder when the children escaped. Now he could hardly walk and had this long, awful journey ahead of him. Away from his darkness. Away from his home. How much medicine could he bring? Should he stop and make more?

He was gasping already. Even reaching the top of the ladder exhausted him. He would make them pay all right. That boy and girl would suffer for frightening him. They would suffer, above all, for disobeying him. He had left rules to be obeyed, and he would punish anyone who disobeyed.

He'd get there. Yes. He'd get there and punish them all. First he had to get more supplies. Once he had supplies, he decided, he could go up to those kids and make them suffer for what they'd done. Then they'd all be sorry. More than sorry.

CHAPTER 8

Prisoners

I T WAS the kind of entertainment Dan could never have imagined — a chance to play judge and jury. He decided that he would hold a trial to convict Han and Ben of endangering Mothership and would then sentence and punish them for their acts. They were marched down to the play area, their hands tied behind their backs, and Dan stood before them as he brought his version of their case before the others.

"Jones always told us," he began, waving the sound gun around menacingly, "and all you have to do is listen to Gus if you want to know about Mothership. We're here to bring the treasures back to Earth and carry on the names of the heroes. Now we don't know how much damage Han and Ben have done but they are trying to make up stories of an attack from Jones so it must be serious. Jones of all people! He's the one who took care of us. He's the one who's gone to Earth to make all things ready for us."

He stared at Luke and smiled.

"So this is what I say we decide." His voice could hardly contain his delight. "I say the sentence is that I give ten blasts of the sound gun to Han and ten blasts to Ben."

"It's all my fault," Luke announced to the others. He was sweating with fear. "Han and Ben didn't cause any harm, and no one would've known they had gone if I hadn't raised the alarm."

"You're a fool," Dan said, "and I've decided that from now on — to keep you out of trouble — I'm going to make you my slave. You'll be like my dog."

Only Fay dared to speak out.

"You can't hurt them like that," she protested, "you don't know what the sound gun does. All those shots might kill Han and Ben — and what happened wasn't Luke's fault."

Dan pointed the gun directly at Fay and walked towards her as he talked.

"Are you going to stop me, Fay?" he hissed.

"When we get back to Earth I'm going to tell on you," she answered defiantly. Dan hadn't thought of that. He couldn't risk doing something to Han and Ben that would get him into trouble when they all arrived back on Earth. He paused, trying to think of a smart answer to Fay's threat. Finally he turned away in anger. He walked to Han and Ben and pointed the gun between Ben's eyes.

"Han and Ben will be punished," he repeated, "and anyone who goes out of bounds or helps anyone go out of bounds will be punished."

"Time for lunch. Time for lunch," the recorded voice declared from the speakers. Relieved to have a chance to consider the situation, Dan seized on this excuse.

"Court adjourned," he announced, just like he'd heard in one of the films. "Tie the prisoners to their bunks. Jim and Gus stand guard over them. I'll decide a punishment later."

As Dan walked away he turned to Luke and grinned.

"Luke — come," he said. Luke bowed his head and

followed Dan. He glanced at Fay and she looked sadly back, as if sharing his misery.

* * * *

Ben was exhausted by all that had happened. There was so much to try to understand, and so many more questions. The others had eventually left Han and Ben alone in the sleeping quarters, firmly tied up to their bunks. Escape was impossible and, worse still for Ben, he couldn't even read his Huck Finn book which he felt under his pillow.

They were left alone with their fears and questions. The noise from the play area drifted up through the corridor. The others were carrying on with their routines in spite of the warnings. Ben lifted his head to see Han.

"Why, Han. Why would we be cargo?"

"I don't know," she said wearily, "I've always reckoned that there was something about us being born that wasn't part of the plan. I keep trying to imagine what things would be like if Mothership wasn't damaged. I bet we wouldn't be here. I bet this ship would still be empty — except for the crew — and travelling through space much faster."

"But going where?" Ben asked "and where has Mothership been? What do we believe anymore?"

"I don't know. I don't understand," Han sighed. "We need to see more of the ship. I need to get access to all the computer files."

They talked little after that but neither could sleep. They were too busy trying to plan their next move.

* * * *

When Dan led the others into the sleeping quarters, Han and Ben braced themselves for trouble. Instead, Dan ignored them and called Luke to follow him.

"You'll sleep on the floor beside my bed, like a good dog," he announced, "and Ike — you sleep in the bunk under Ben, in case he tries anything stupid."

The others wouldn't talk to Han and Ben, and ignored their efforts to convince them of danger. When the lights dimmed, the stillness was broken by the sound of Luke sobbing and Dan shouting at him to be quiet.

Ben's eyes grew heavy. He was tired and confused, and his brain felt dull and aching. He eventually gave way to sleep, slumping back on the bunk with his arms splayed by the cords. In his sleep he had a strange dream.

He saw the face of the woman again. Very close to him, smiling warmly. It was Mommy. She picked him up and cradled him close to her warm, soft body. He felt safe and loved. Then in an instant her smile vanished and he was looking up into the mad eyes of Jones. Jones let him go and pointed down at him saying: "You're dead." Ben fell through endless space.

He snapped awake and looked around in the faint light. Stretching, with a slight creak of his bunk, he looked to Han. She was awake and gave him a little smile. Ben smiled back and closed his eyes. Soon he was asleep once more.

Han remained awake, trying to think up a plan. She reckoned that if she could get free she could take the access keypad from the end door at the bottom level and use it to fix the one to the control deck. That way she could get to the guns and perhaps use the master computer to counter any attempts Jones might make to sabotage their life support systems. She struggled to free herself from the cords, but to no avail. Eventually she, too, fell asleep.

Everyone was in deep sleep when Han was woken by a hand pressed to her mouth. It was Fay, who silently untied her and crept back to her bunk.

Han slipped across to Ben. Ike stirred in the bunk underneath. She could not risk discovery to set Ben free —

better for one of them to get away than neither of them. She slipped out of the sleeping quarters, and sprinted down the levels to the end door.

As she examined the access keypad a green light flashed. Han was startled — this meant the link was in use. It had to be Jones. Because she was unarmed and had no hope of convincing the others that Jones was dangerous, her only hope was to get out of sight as quickly as possible.

She hid in the doorway of a classroom and waited. Would he come armed? Would he hurt or kill any of the others? The fact that he had lied and lived in hiding from them on Mothership was nothing compared to the fact that he had surely lost his mind. Such a wild man seemed capable of doing anything.

Finally the link door opened. Han heard a dragging noise, and didn't dare peep out. Jones limped into view clutching a small black bag to his chest. He was pale and sweating and looked wild-eyed.

Jones slowly passed the door where Han hid. She was just starting to breathe a sigh of relief when he halted and turned back. Quickly she crouched back into the shadows.

Jones stopped at the door of the classroom and chuckled quietly. Had he noticed her? Han froze to the spot. At last Jones turned and walked away along the corridor. Han lay on the floor for several minutes just trying to calm her racing heart.

CHAPTER 9

New Order

WERE they hiding? They hadn't fixed the link, so the two Jones caught must have made their way down to him on their own somehow. They were still kids — but if they gathered to fight him... He cursed the stupid rule about having no weapons on the ship — just those pathetic sound guns up on control deck.

He was so tired and the pain was like a knife stuck in his brain. Curse them. They would pay dearly for their mistake. He was too sick to be doing all this — but since they now knew he was still on the ship he had to find out what they were up to and what else they'd discovered in his absence.

Moving up along the winding corridor, the place was all too familiar to him. He remembered a time when he used to jog along these corridors — was that really him? Did the person who was Jones before that terrible moment years ago still exist as the person dragging himself along the corridor now?

He stepped into the deserted play area and was surprised to find that only some of the chairs were broken and there wasn't very much litter. He was surprised, too, that there was no sign of the kids. Was it possible that they obeyed the orders he had programmed to tell them when to sleep and wake?

He moved on up past the feeding area — which was in a much worse state and was littered with old tubes and containers spilling around one of the refuse chutes. Again there was no sign of anyone.

Sweat was trickling down his face from the effort. All he could think of now was getting through to the control deck — away from these accursed children — and then having some of his medicine. As he finally approached the top end of the corridor, he cried out at the sight before him. The access keypad for the link was smashed to pieces!

He slumped back against the wall, starting to feel trapped again. The ship was closing in on him. If he couldn't get away through the link then he had to take his medicine. He began shivering as he settled down on the floor and opened the bag. The medicine would make him better. Then he would go back and find out who had broken the keypad and punish them... or simply punish them all. He wanted to kill them all. He wanted to destroy the ship. What did he care? He pulled back his sleeve. The sweat was trickling into his stinging eyes.

* * * *

Han made her way down to the life support deck through the repaired link. She went quickly past the modules and their skeletons and reached the cargo deck.

Jones probably had lived alone in his hovel, but Han

felt very afraid there alone and unarmed. She made her way through the crates in the semi-darkness and found an exit which wound down to an area which was different from other connections between decks.

Instead of a small link entrance to the next deck, there was a tall bay door. Facing this was a row of spider-like vehicles with forklifts in front and metal claws to the sides and rear. These vehicles were topped by half sphere windows for all-round visibility, and a small hatch leading inside.

Han climbed into one and quickly realised it was a pressurised cabin with its own air supply. She engaged the computer controls and followed the procedure for passing through the bay doors to the transport deck. As she triggered up the vehicle's silent engine, a soft alarm instructed her to strap into the safety harness on the seat. With some difficulty she then steered the vehicle to crawl towards the bay door which opened to reveal a tall and broad tunnel no more than thirty metres long. The door closed behind her.

The vehicle then sprang gently forward into the gravity gap and floated down the tunnel. Han became weightless in the seat and the harness held her firmly in place. The vehicle set down its claws at the other end of the gravity gap and approached the door which opened to reveal an incredible sight.

The transport deck was one gigantic chamber with three types of space ship lined up at either side of a short runway. This runway led to an iris shaped wall at the other end of the deck.

Two big ships — each would easily carry a hundred people — stood beside four smaller craft. Three one-person space pods stood in a launch area made to carry four such ships.

Han drove towards one of the big ships, scanning the options on her vehicle's computer controls. A diagram of the ship came up on her screen with instructions for opening the entry panel to the main deck. She steered her vehicle into a a bright chamber, the walls of which were lined with untouched spacesuits. The suits bore the familiar crest of a crescent edge to a sphere and the letters 'UWPA'.

Craving an explanation for all these space craft, Han climbed out of her vehicle and used the ship's elevator.

This brought her to an area lined with seats which was like the space shuttles she had seen in one of the school video discs about the history of space travel. There were no living quarters so it was obviously built for short flights. She walked past the pristine seats and through a door into the cockpit. Sitting into one of the pilot seats, she activated the ship computer.

The screen showed a programmed flight path which assumed a planetary orbit by Mothership, set to bring the shuttle to a safe landing. The information was plain and simple. But then Han saw the destination. The planet was not Earth. The programmed destination was called Planet Ararat.

* * * *

Jones woke from the stupor which had swallowed him up. He felt better. His head was not as clear as when he first started taking the medicine but he could stand up. There was no choice — he would have to go to the children and find out what had happened to the access keypad. Holding his black bag close to his chest Jones returned to the sleeping quarters. He looked around in the dim light and could make out bodies in some of the bunks. If they were asleep he would go first to his own bed and rest awhile.

As he came into his room he saw two figures, one asleep in the bed, the other asleep on the floor and tied to the leg of the bed. He peered into the face of the one on the bed. This boy was fat and snored slightly. Jones grabbed him by the neck and lifted up the suddenly screeching boy. "What're you doing here?" Jones barked. He flung the boy back.

"Help! Please!" Dan squealed.

"Ben?" Jones asked, leaning towards him. Dan shook his head. "Dan. The other white boy. You got bigger than I expected. What are you doing in my bed? Don't you know you kids aren't allowed in the adult quarters?"

Jones turned and sneered at Luke.

"Luke, isn't it? Still a runt. He bosses you around?"

While Jones' attention was distracted, Dan reached for the sound gun. Jones caught him in the act and struck him across the face with the back of his fist. Dan's head knocked against the wall, dazing him.

"Bad boy!" Jones snarled, dragging Dan off the bed. But then he became weak and staggered back. The exertion of pushing Dan around was quickly proving too much. He fell on the bed as the fever finally took over. In what seemed like the far distance he heard Luke cry out to the others, screaming with fear and panic. Then, through a cloud, young faces rushed in as the lights in his head swam around. One by one their contorted faces appeared above his bleary eyes.

Their confusion was plain. They couldn't believe or understand. Jones was supposed to be back on Earth.

* * * *

At first Han cried out. The idea was like a blow to her chest, and her heart pounded. She fled the shuttle and the transport deck. She did not want to believe the terrible truth uncovered by her own logic and hunger for knowledge.

All she could think of was getting back to Jones' hut in the hope of finding something hidden there that would deny the dreadful facts.

Jones' place was a stinking mess of old clothes and food containers. Among the video discs piled around the TV she found a silver cover on which was etched the words "United World Project Ark". She picked it up and ran her finger across the words as pieces of the puzzle came together in her head.

"UWPA — United World Project Ark," she whispered to herself. It was so clear now — the deception had been greater than anyone could have imagined.

She took the disc and inserted it in the player. Settling down on her haunches she stared at the TV screen.

CHAPTER 10

The Project

"Han was right," Fay said, "Jones didn't go to Earth." "What do we do with him?" Luke asked. Gus dared to move closer. He touched Jones' face.

"He's sick. We have to take care of him."

"But Han thinks he wants to kill us," Fay said.

"Do we take him prisoner?" Eve asked.

Dan got slowly to his feet as his senses returned.

"Get out of my way," he boomed. As he looked down at Jones he was filled with confusion. Glimmers of ideas came and went. To Dan's way of thinking there could be only one truth.

"He came back," Dan said finally. "He returned from Earth for some reason and something went wrong. Maybe his ship broke down getting here. We have to take care of him."

Outside, tied to his bunk, Ben called to the others to tell him what was going on. Fay went to him.

"Jones is back," she whispered. Ben instantly thought of Han and looked for her.

"Han is gone," Fay said. "They haven't realised yet. Ben — listen to me — this is like the feeling I get sometimes about Mothership. I've felt there are ghosts on the ship. Warning us. Telling me to warn everyone else. Ben — are we in danger?"

"Yes. Yes." Ben was impatient. "Please. You have to free me. Who knows what Jones will do?"

Fay looked around just as Jim and Eve came into the room.

"Do you believe me now?" Ben asked them. Dan came pushing through and glared at Ben.

"Jones is sick. You found him and he was sick and you just ran away from him." Dan's face was red with rage "He'll punish you for what you've done. You'll see. Now that Jones is here everything is going to change."

*   *   *   *

An image of Planet Earth came on screen, just as Han had seen it in the school video discs. A lush, green and blue planet, it basked in the glow of the Sun as it glided majestically through space. But then the image started to change. The clouds that swirled around the face of the planet became thicker and more prevalent. The land outline began to change — first shrinking, then growing.

The screen showed images of life on the planet — first showing scenes Han was familiar with: houses, streets, fields and rivers. But then came an increasing number of natural disasters caused by fierce weather. People struggled through thick snow on the streets of cities. Ships were stranded in frozen seas. A sombre voice explained what was happening.

"The human race has made many ecological mistakes which have damaged the environment of the planet. The nations of the world reacted too late to repair the damage. Having responded as best it could to survive our mistreatment, the planet itself has now reacted to the global warming we caused by entering its natural cycle of recuperation and rejuvenation. Planet Earth has entered a new ice age. Despite the best efforts of our scientists we have not been able to prevent the dawning of this new ice age. All attempts to shorten the cycle have failed also, and it is now believed that our planet will be largely ice-bound for at least another sixty thousand years."

The face of the planet was being contorted as ice drifts annihilated towns and cities. Gigantic roads, ten lanes wide, that once stretched across countries, now zigzagged in crunched earth surrounded by ice flows. Life for the people was one of famine and misery. There were scenes of massive exodus through bitter storms to barren landscapes that could offer little hope of survival.

"The best our technology can do for us is to offer some shelter for the fraction of the planet's population still remaining," the voice continued, "the human race has developed through its capacity to survive by adaptation. We have built new societies to suit our changing world."

Han was seeing something for the first time: Earth's civilisation surviving underground. Cities were underground and people were shown living in tiny cells. It seemed an even more miserable existence than that on Mothership. Even though Han and the others were confined on the ship, they at least had space to play and roam. The people in these colonies reminded Han of pictures she'd seen of ant hills.

"Although our population has been so greatly reduced, we cannot sustain the resources necessary to ensure the survival of even these small colonies. The nations of the planet must choose whether to risk the end of the human race, should the struggle to survive on Earth fail, or to look to a new home. This reality has led to the greatest endeavour in human history: United World Project Ark."

Scientists worked to design a giant space ship. Finally a model was chosen - Han recognised it as Mothership. Space shuttles brought materials into orbit while workers on a space station above Earth built the decks of the ship. The voice explained the plan.

"At great sacrifice to all nations, by combining the best of our technology with what remains of our materials, the United World is aiming to complete a daring plan. Space probe astronomy has identified a planet further inside the galaxy which is virtually a twin of Planet Earth. Study suggests that there may be no advanced life forms on the planet as there are no indications of centres of population."

Music surged as the completed Mothership floated above the white Planet Earth.

"The bible tells of another time in the history of civilisation when it was necessary for humankind to save some spark of itself to last through a natural disaster. Noah's Ark stored all life during the Flood. When the flood ceased in Noah's time, his Ark struck ground on Mount Ararat and from there life was rekindled to begin anew. We have seized this opportunity for a second chance in the same manner as Noah in biblical times. The seed of mankind will be carried to the planet we now call Ararat."

The film went on to show how the cream of world knowledge was gathered to make the lessons that Han had studied in the classrooms. Cargo was launched from Earth and loaded.

"The UWP Ark will travel with a six person crew on this hundred-and-two-year mission. The crew will operate ten year shifts, with one couple in charge of the mission while the others hibernate. In the nineteenth year of the project, the two hundred children will be born and all six crew will tend to them as the ship approaches the planet.

"By the time the children are twelve years old, the UWP Ark will be orbiting Planet Ararat and all the livestock will have hatched. This new seed of the human race will then be landed on the planet to start a new chapter in the story of humankind."

Han stared at the film of the crew in training. The crew — three men and three women — posed together in one shot. They were obviously couples, perhaps married. She recognised Jones. He looked so young and so happy. He and the woman beside him embraced, smiling. So there was once a time when Jones wasn't mad — just as there was once a time when Han thought that there would be hope for them all if only the truth about Mothership could be found.

"These are the brave men and women who will carry and protect the seed of the human race. David Aiko, Indira Ranjani, Dmitry Novomeysky, Anika Mbata, and Ken and Helen Jones. Into their hands the world entrusts this greatest and most important of all missions."

Han felt a strange taste on her lips. She touched her face and it was wet. Tears were trickling down her face. For the first time since she was a child Han was crying.

She curled into a ball on the floor and sobbed. It seemed there could be nothing else to do but cry — for herself, the few survivors stranded on Mothership, and the people on Earth who had sacrificed so much for what they believed to be one last chance of maintaining the human race.

Han even wept for Jones. He and the woman on the video disc seemed so happy and enthusiastic. They were husband and wife, setting off on the greatest adventure in the history of the human race. What had happened to the dream? What had gone so terribly wrong with Mothership?

* * * *

A boy leaned over Jones, dabbing his face with a cloth. He looked pallid and miserable. Jones reached out and grabbed him by the throat, squeezing hard. The boy started to croak, arms flailing and eyes bulging. Jones wondered if this meant the boy was real — or at least more real than the demons that haunted his nightmares and memories.

"Get my bag," Jones said, "my bag. Medicine. I have a kit. Needle. Get them."

The boy grabbed the bag from the side of the bed, opened it, and took out the needle. Jones released the choking grip and the boy slumped to the floor.

"Now go away," Jones said, clutching the needle.

Luke crawled to the door.

* * * *

Han forced herself to stop crying. Discovering the truth about Mothership was both a shock and a responsibility. She had to think clearly. She had to believe there was a solution.

Rooting through the heaps of junk and medicine in Jones' hovel, she found discs labelled 'Crew Reports'. They were not the same design as the other video discs. Han was sure they were made to be used in the computer on master control deck.

These reports should tell exactly what had happened to the ship and in turn might lead to some way of repairing the damage. If it couldn't be repaired, Han knew that they would be doomed to live out their lives on this drifting space coffin.

* * * *

Luke, pale with fright, staggered out to the sleeping quarters where Ben was still tied to his bunk.

"Jones is awake," he whispered.

"Are you okay?" Ben was afraid for his friend.

"Yeah sure," Luke said vacantly. "Jones is very sick. He's got his own medicine."

Ike sat up.

"Go tell Dan," he ordered, and Luke walked away.

He went down the winding corridor to the play area where Dan had ordered a frenzied tidying up. He wanted Mothership spick and span for Jones' inspection. Dan was terrified of making Jones angry. He wanted to be able to line them up like an efficient crew in front of Jones to show that he'd kept perfect order on Mothership all the time Jones was away.

Ben was surprised when Jones emerged from the bedroom. The man looked at least a little tidier — and saner — than when they had first seen him in his cargo deck hovel. His hair was pulled back from his haggard face. His hand trembled as he scratched his deep black beard. Jones reminded Ben of Huckleberry Finn's father — he had that same demented nature.

"Untie him," Jones ordered Ike as he reached the bunk. Ike obeyed nervously, and Ben sat up to look into Jones' eyes. Jones was mad — no doubt about it — yet Ben felt defiant rather than afraid.

Jones' scowled and then laughed.

"You've got guts, haven't you," he boomed. "You dare look me straight in the eye. Where's the girl — Han, wasn't it?"

"Han isn't here."

Just as quickly, Jones became dour and angry.

"Well find her. I want you all together."

The others arrived, led by Dan. Jones turned to him.

"I heard you were awake," Dan said, "do you want anything? Food?"

"I want to talk to you all," Jones said. "I want to find out what's been going on. And I want to break the neck of whoever it was smashed up the access keypad."

"The keypad?" Dan's mind raced to hide his guilt. "Han

did it, and now she's disappeared. She's fallen out of Mothership."

Jones slapped him across the face.

"You're stupid. I can't bear stupidity." He turned to the rest of the group. They were all terrified. "I want to see you all lined up. I want to see what the years have done to you."

They started to shuffle into a line, as if they were soldiers on parade.

"In alphabetical order," he said, "like we named you. Anne, Ben, Con, Dan, Eve, Fay, Gus, Han, Ike, Jim, Kay, and Luke."

Eleven stood there. Jones swaggered like a pirate captain from one of the video discs.

"You're probably all wondering why I'm here and where I've been. Well I have a story to tell, and I have changes to make, and you're all going to learn about the new rules on Mothership."

CHAPTER 11

The Return

"CHILDREN. My children. The last time I saw you was when you were six years old," Jones said. "I didn't expect to see you again until we were all back on Earth — but things didn't happen that way. The ship I set off in broke down and I just managed to survive until Mothership reached me. So now I'm sick, you see, and you have to take care of me."

He looked at their faces. Most were afraid of him. All but Ben believed him.

"Excuse me sir," Jim said hesitantly. Jones stared at him, first scowling and then smiling.

"You have a question?"

"Yes sir. Could you tell us — how far away from Earth are we?"

Jones thought about this for a moment.

"Not so far," he finally replied. "Any other questions?"

"I have a question," Ben said. Jones stared at him. Ben could sense the danger.

"Ask it." Somehow, Ben felt strong enough to stare right back as he spoke.

"How badly damaged is Mothership?"

"No!" Jones screamed, "No! You will not ask those kind of questions! That's just stupid talk from stupid kids and I won't hear any of it! Dan! Come here!"

Shaking with fear, Dan obeyed.

"There's going to be order on Mothership," Jones barked, sneering at Ben. "I will be obeyed at all times, and there'll be no going out of bounds, and no stupid questions!" By now Jones was red with rage, the veins on his neck jutting out like snakes under his skin. "You're going to find Han. That's the first thing to do. And then I'm going to punish her, and you'll see that no one gets away with disobeying me."

Jones turned to Dan and grinned as he took the sound gun off the boy's shoulder.

"I didn't do anything!" Dan pleaded. Jones waved the gun in his face and Dan seemed close to tears. "It's not my fault! I swear! I didn't know anything about the keypad."

"Shut up!" Jones roared and Dan became silent. Then Jones handed the gun back to Dan, who couldn't understand what was happening.

"Shoot Ben," Jones said, "for running away from me when he could have helped."

The others stood aside. For Dan, it was a dream come true. He looked into Ben's eyes for some sign of fear, but there was none. He aimed squarely at Ben's chest and smiled as he pulled the trigger. Ben was tossed back across the room with a force so strong he felt his ribs were going to crack open. He lay on the floor racked with pain, but he would not give either Jones or Dan the pleasure of seeing him cry.

"Dan is my bodyguard," Jones announced. "Luke and Fay — the smallest ones — will be my servants. The rest of you will do as you're told. That's the way things are going to be on Mothership. I'm not bringing a bunch of rowdy, disobedient idiots back to Earth."

Suddenly, Jones went pale. His hands began to tremble and he looked around the room as if it were fading away from him.

"I need my medicine now," he mumbled, "take me back to my room."

Dan, Luke and Jim went to him. Propping him up as his feet gave way, they brought him back to the sleeping quarters.

"You can see he's mad," Ben said to the others when Jones was gone, "we have to do something to stop him or who knows what he'll do."

"I agree with Ben," Fay said, "I can sense his evil. I know he's the one I've been warned about in my dreams."

But the others wouldn't listen.

"You were so cruel," Con said, "finding him, sick and weak, and running away from him instead of helping. Anyone with a heart would have helped him. You deserved your punishment."

"You didn't see what we saw," Ben insisted, "he was living down there. He never left Mothership. And he lied to us about everything."

"We have to do what Jones says," Anne concluded, and the others agreed.

"Just because he's a grown-up?" Ben got slowly to his feet. "Don't you think it's strange that he lied to us about the rest of Mothership?"

"But it's out of bounds," Kay argued, "maybe he had to tell us those stories."

"And how come he's still not admitting that there's something wrong with the ship? I saw the damage with my own two eyes."

Dan came back to the room and yelled when he saw the others gathered around Ben.

"No one listens to Ben! Anyone who listens to Ben will

be shot by me! Now tie him to his bunk and get back to work tidying up Mothership!"

* * * *

Han rested in the cargo deck until she reckoned it was time for bed on the living deck, then she set out on her mission. She had decided on a clear plan of action and was determined to see it through. In a small back pack she carried the Project video disc and flight report discs she had found in Jones' hut.

As she passed through the life support deck, with its skeletons and lost dreams of a new future for mankind, she felt very alone and afraid. She wished that Ben could be with her, so that her fight wouldn't seem so daunting. Ben had been the only one to question life on Mothership, and she now regretted not taking the risk to free him.

She made her way up the winding corridor of the life support deck to use the link to the living deck which Jones had repaired. As she drew near the end door, however, she heard it opening. It had to be Jones, or some of the others sent to find her. There was no hiding place in the corridor, so she rushed back to the shattered doorway of Maintenance One. Blinded by the change from the brightness to this large dark area, she shone her torch looking for a hiding place. There was none. Crouching down just inside the door, she waited for the enemy.

The light from the corridor suddenly cast a long shadow into the room. A figure glanced around and stepped in. Had only one person come to hunt her? Then it must be Jones. If she attacked suddenly and hard enough she might overcome him. Gathering all her courage, Han dived on him, fists flailing.

"Han! Han!"

She recognised the voice.

"Ben!" They were so happy to see each other their grips turned to hugs.

"Fay untied me!" Ben said.

"And me — she's on our side."

"Jones is mad — he's taken over up there."

"Ben — I'm sorry for not helping you escape with me," Han said, "I should've risked it."

"It's okay. You made the right choice," Ben reassured her, "the main thing was that one of us escaped Jones. He won't admit there's anything wrong with Mothership. And he's out for your blood."

"I've learned more, Ben. An awful lot more. The truth gets more complicated."

"Jones says he's bringing us back to Earth."

Han looked at Ben, sorry for the shock he was about to receive. He was still full of smiles — so delighted to be with her.

"Ben," she said, holding his arm, "Mothership is headed away from Earth. We were the seed of mankind being sent to another planet."

Ben stared at her. He didn't want to believe.

"We have to get into the control deck," she continued, "then I'll have access to all the information. We'll know the whole truth."

Ben laughed shakily.

"Didn't seem like much of a home planet anyway," he said. Han wondered if Ben could cry, but he just sighed and spoke quietly. "I guess it's like you said. It's better to know."

"Be brave," Han whispered.

"I'll try," Ben replied.

"No. No." Han smiled. "My mistake. You are brave."

Ben felt he could be honest with her about how he felt.

"I'm scared, Han. Really scared. Since all this started, it's like I feel in danger all the time. It doesn't seem the same with you — don't you have any fear?" It was the first time Han felt close enough to anyone to share the truth.

"You'll never believe what happened to me when I found out about our destination," she said, "I cried. I cried, Ben. Do you ever cry?"

"No one cries on Mothership," Ben replied, "except for Luke — and he gets bullied all the worst for it."

"Ben, I'm probably the most frightened person on this ship," Han whispered, "but I can't bear the dread of waiting for the worst. So I use my fear to go on and on until it happens. That's my secret Ben — I just keep hunting down my fear."

"Well any bravery gets tested now," Ben said, looking towards the tall air supply shaft beyond them. "Since the access keypad has been bashed up we can only get to the control deck by travelling along the air supply pipe. And I reckon it's safer to get into it here than through the living deck in case we get caught. If Jones gets us before we can convince the rest of what's really happening, we're finished."

They went to the pipe and climbed up to enter the broken hatch. Inside, the rungs stretched above and below them into icy darkness.

It had been difficult enough before to bypass one link from the bottom of the living deck to the top of the life support deck. Now they both had to go all the way up past the living deck as well. As they climbed, their hands became more and more numb until Ben used his like claws to hang on each rung as he pulled himself up.

Eventually they reached the maintenance hatch at the bottom level of the control deck. It was easily opened and they climbed out of the pipe to open the wall panelling which led them into the corridor.

Pausing only briefly, despite their exhaustion, they marched up past the computer rooms and took the elevator that overlooked the cold fusion reactor. All the while they were silent. Their only thoughts were of unlocking the truth that now seemed so close.

Finally they reached the master control room.

Han went immediately to the main computer console and, opening her back pack, used the disc she believed would contain all mission files. She summoned up the Mission Flight Plan — something which before had always given the response 'Access Denied'. The computer purred and a graphic display evolved on the screen plotting the exact course. Ben studied it, but couldn't understand.

"What does it all mean?" He asked.

"Planet Earth," Han pointed to the start of the journey, "Mothership was built in Earth orbit and launched from there. It was supposed to be a hundred and two year mission. This is where we are now."

Ben judged the distance.

"It's about a third of the way," he said.

"Yes but look," Han pointed out date references to the journey's progress, "we were here thirteen years ago and we're here now."

The distance between the two points was hardly a fraction compared to that travelled in the first twenty seven years.

"Mothership is barely moving," Han said. She spun the chair around to face another screen. She inserted the first mission report disc and in a moment the screen came to life showing the smiling face of a young man.

"Officer David Aiko reporting. Dateline thirty days A.E. — that's After Earth, as we've decided to date things. Well anyway, you've got the time code on the disc so why not. Project Ark is running perfectly smoothly. As all initial tests have been carried out and all checks confirm status AOK, the other four members of the crew have now gone into suspended animation while myself and Officer Ranjani take on this first ten years of minding the store. Ready now for monitor file store. Three, two, one..."

In less than a second there was a flicker of images of all the monitors on Mothership showing the status of all the decks. Han removed that disc and flicked through to find the last one. She looked at Ben. They knew this would tell them what disaster had befallen Mothership.

She inserted the disc and a woman's face came up on screen. The woman looked tired and shocked. A memory bolted to life in Ben's mind. He knew that face. He had seen it before. He had touched it.

The woman stared from the screen and began to speak.

CHAPTER 12

Damage Report

"**O**FFICER Helen Jones reporting. Dateline twenty — seven years two-hundred and ninety- eight days A.E. Mothership has been struck by an uncharted, unidentified meteor shower. The shower carried an ultra-velocity electron charge and its impact caused severe damage to the life support deck as well as other damage to be catalogued. The damage to the life support deck is extreme. As a result of an enormous flood of voltage through it crew members Aiko, Ranjani, Mbata and Novomeysky have all lost their lives."

She paused for a moment, struggling to regain calmness in her voice. Han listened intently to her words, but Ben stared at the face on the screen.

"Han. Han," he said, "I know her. I've seen her. I used to dream about that face."

"Ssshhh," Han said as Helen continued.

"I am recording these reports as a matter of formality but they cannot at present be transmitted because all external transmitters have been completely destroyed. Our first task is to make the ship safe. A secondary task will be the fitting of some alternative form of communication.

"Ken and I are working around the clock just trying to calculate the damage. We have reduced our travel speed to factor one because of the danger of stress tearing the damaged deck apart. We also have reason to believe that all livestock cells have been contaminated and that the power supply to the life storage units may have been damaged beyond repair. As a precaution, we have decided to begin the hatching of twelve of the cargo: six boys and six girls in a cross-section of racial types. While there is no logic to this in terms of the original plan, we can't take a chance on being able to get Project Ark back on course for the original time scale."

They watched the following entries, some made by Helen and some by Jones himself. One entry announced the birth of the twelve babies. There were shots of the twelve being tended by Helen Jones.

"Mommy," Ben said. The word came out without his even meaning to say it. "I do remember. I remember her face looking into mine."

"I think I remember too — I'm not sure. But where is she now?" Han wondered, "what happened?"

There were reports about the growth of the children and work to repair Mothership. The woman came on screen again, this time looking very grim.

"Two years and ninety days have passed since the collision. All stored cells are dead despite our efforts to repair the storage unit on the life support deck. The babies show no sign of disorder, but there was definite radioactive contamination at the time of the collision. All of the simple repairs have now been completed, but we cannot resume normal flight speed until we seal the wide gash on the exterior of the ship in the lower region of the life support deck.

"Ken and I will now set out in pods and hope to fit a cover he has made which will isolate the exposed section of the ship's main power cable. If this is successful, we may regain full power supply on the ship and safely weld a new covering over the ship's ripped hull. We will record this mission for the file."

Han and Ben watched the story unfold.

Ken and Helen set out from the transport deck in two pods. Ken's carried in its grips a long tube made of a mirror-like, plastic substance he had formed in the laboratory. They travelled up along the vast hull of Mothership, past the cargo deck with the signs of repair work already completed there, until they reached the gaping wound at the side of the life support deck.

Getting the tube inside the gap was difficult to manoeuvre and they tried several times before succeeding. Part of the main power cable had been sliced away, leaving a gap of about three metres along one side of it with the frayed strands sparking at either end. Ken and Helen faced the task of trying to fit each end of the shattered cable into the tube before sealing it.

They docked side by side near the cable and Ken released the tubing to float free. The pods then grabbed one end each and began a sideways movement to cover the far end of the cable. They succeeded, and went on to start the much more difficult task of covering the end from which some charge was still being released.

As they made the first attempt, the end of the tube pushed one of the cable strands into contact with another and a flash of heat melted part of the tubing.

"That can't happen," Ken said over his transmitter. "We can't risk distorting the end of the tube."

"We'll do it. We'll do it," Helen said evenly. "Practice makes perfect." They moved back and made another approach. As they neared the cable again the strands made contact and there was another heat flash. Another part of the tubing was distorted.

"There's only one thing for it," Helen decided. "I'm going out. I'll circle the loose strands with a length of safety cable and tighten them up enough to fit inside the tube without being jostled by it."

"That's far too risky," Ken protested. "We can't do it."

"We've got to do it, Ken. Stand by."

"Please Helen." But Jones' words fell on deaf ears. In a short while, Helen emerged from her pod in a jet-propelled spacesuit, carrying a lasso of cable.

"Just call me Annie Oakley, the queen of the wild west," she said. Ken chuckled nervously.

"Be careful with the round-up."

Helen expertly fed out the slim cable as she circled the strands. Then she tightened the stray bunch until it was neat without actually bringing any of the strands in contact with each other.

"You can start moving in now," she instructed.

"Get clear first," Ken said.

"No point. While I'm here I might as well hang around to give a nudge if it's needed."

"Be careful, Helen. Please."

Slowly he brought the tubing forward. His aim was good, and as he drew closer all was well.

"Everything's looking AOK," Helen announced.

It was the last moment before contact, and the steadily approaching tube was about to start swallowing the cables.

"Wait, hold it," Helen said, and she ducked down suddenly to look beneath where she noticed a loose strand. In that instant, the tube made contact with the cable and caught Helen's hand in between. She cried out and Ken called her name. He instantly reversed thrust, but in so doing there was a jerk which snapped the noose of the safety cable. The sparking strands flicked back and struck Helen. With a flash of light she disintegrated in a plume of bright dust that sprayed out into infinity.

"Helen! Helen! Helen! Helen!" The word was repeated again and again until the screen turned to white noise and

Han and Ben were staring at ghost grey reflections of themselves. There were no more reports. Only Jones knew the rest of the story, and he had never committed it to disc.

Han turned to Ben. Her face was contorted with pain and anger.

"We're going back to the others," she said coldly. "But there's something we need to get before we go any further. Follow me."

CHAPTER 13

Proof

JONES woke to the feel of a sound gun pressed against his neck. He looked up into the angry faces of Han and Ben. Both had guns. Both were very ready to use them.

For Han and Ben, the time had come. The truth was clear. Jones' lies had left them wandering through space with nothing but stories to live for.

"We saw Helen," Ben said. The very mention of her name sent a shiver through Jones.

"We know the truth about Project Ark," Han added. "We have the disc to show Dan and the others. Now it's time for you to help us instead of tricking us."

"Why didn't you fix the cable?" Ben asked.

"I... I couldn't," Jones stuttered. He wondered if this was some new nightmare, more vivid than the many that had haunted him through the long years since his wife's death. "In the accident the tube became too distorted."

"You could've tried another way," Han said.

"I couldn't do it," Jones snapped. Tears started welling in his bleary eyes as memories he couldn't bear rushedclearly into his mind. "I couldn't go on. Not without Helen. Not without hope."

"You gave up," Han said. Jones' eyes flitted from one accusing face to the other.

"Did you tell the people on Earth?" Ben asked, "are they sending help?"

Jones laughed.

"What do you think we do? Pick up a phone? We're too far away to be in any direct contact now. Our flight was being tracked by a space probe, but all surface antennae on this ship were destroyed on impact with that storm."

"Didn't you do anything to let Earth know?"

"We were going to — we couldn't repair the ship." Jones became feverish. He didn't want to think or talk. "Helen would have launched a pod which we'd set up like a beacon repeating our emergency message. She reckoned eventually someone would pick up the signal and search for us."

"You could've turned back," Han persisted. "Why didn't you do that?"

"I didn't think it mattered!" Jones replied. "At the speed this ship can manage because of the damage it's over three hundred years to get to Ararat, over a hundred and fifty years to get back to Earth. So the plan is what? To have your descendants arrive on Earth and ask for a bed in the underground hives?"

Han and Ben stared at him in disdain. Faced with choices, he had delayed and done nothing and then had finally withdrawn into his private world.

"Project Ark," he hissed, "the human race messed up one planet, so it decides to move on to another. It was the great mission. We were so proud to be the ones entrusted with carrying Earth's seed to a new home. We were the heroes. But it wasn't to be. And I saw... I saw my friends die, and the seeds decay, and my wife just... just..."

He searched around him for the medicine bag.

"Keep talking," Han demanded.

"No talking. No thinking," he growled, "just leave me alone."

"You made all of us pay for your misery," Han continued. Jones found his bag but Han grabbed it away from him. "You have responsibilities to us and to Project Ark. You have to stop looking back and start looking for a way out!"

"There's no way out! There's no way out!" His fitful breathing turned to sobs and he buried his face in his hands. Han and Ben looked at each other. They almost felt sorry for the man. They had thought he had some devious reason for hiding the truth. But it seemed now it was simply something he couldn't face.

"As the years went by I watched you all growing up — and for what?" he groaned, "I couldn't bear it anymore. So I told you the stories and I went off to live alone so that I wouldn't have to know. Wouldn't have to see your faces as you swallowed the lies." He sneered at them. "But you had to come find me. You had to look for the truth. Well are you happy now you've found it? The truth is that there's no way out. No easy punishment for mankind's crimes. Here we are. The last of the late great human race. We're going to fade away on the biggest, bravest spaceship ever built. There aren't even enough supplies on this ship for the three hundred year journey it would take to reach Ararat and the generations of people who'd grow on this ship, and yet there's nowhere else to go. Nowhere to hide."

He reached out for Han and she was ready to fire her gun.

"I need my medicine," he pleaded.

"Don't move," Han said.

"Or what? You'll shoot me? Kill me? But I'm already dead. I died when Helen died."

Han gave him the black bag. He fumbled through it

and took out a needle and a tube of pale liquid.

"Why didn't you tell us?" Ben felt betrayed.

"Tell the truth?" Jones' laugh became a feverish cough. "Haven't you realised it yet? You'll find it's more than you can bear."

"There has to be a way out," Han said. "There has to be. Somehow."

"For a start, you're going to tell the others what's really happened to Mothership," Ben said.

"So you have twelve panic-stricken kids trapped on a space ship?"

"No," Han snapped, "so we can try to figure a way out. It's our lives and we have the right to decide what we can do."

"You want an option?" Jones snapped, "okay — here's an option. Turn up the power on the reactor. You know what'll happen? This ship will rip in two. Want another option? Okay, try this — XT25. You'll see it in the file — Helen even did some research on it and she was going to do more. It's a planet about a year's travel from where we are now. The scientists called it a wild planet. It's at about the same evolutionary point that Earth was two hundred million years ago. Just you think about that. Think of facing unstable climate, unstable atmosphere, primitive life forms, and zero chances of survival. You think that's an option?" Jones started shouting, his frenzy growing with each word. "The great adventure! The great mission! The great dawn! Mothership! Well here we are. Let the trumpets play and the drums roll, because this is Mothership and we're on the greatest mission that ever was or ever, ever will be!"

Dan burst into the room. The others had been woken by Jones' ranting. He aimed his gun at Ben, but Han fired first and Dan toppled back into the sleeping quarters. The rage Ben felt for his fate, Jones' lies, and their pointless lives flooded up in him as he roared at Dan.

"This time I get you!" Ben yelled, tossing his sound gun to Han.

He lunged forward, landing full force on top of Dan and they rolled along the floor and under a bunk. Dan heaved Ben off him. A row of bunks toppled like dominoes as the two struggled to their feet to lock again in fiery combat.

It was an equal match. Dan was heavier but slower. Ben grappled with him and managed to twist his arm in a painful grip. Dan yelled out in pain, struggling to grab Ben's neck. Jim and Ike were about to intervene when Han aimed her gun at them.

"Don't move," she warned, and they watched in amazement as the fight continued. Han wanted to fire at Dan, but the fighters were too close and she would only stun them both. She called to them to stop, but they ignored her.

Dan managed to grip Ben's neck, squeezing hard so that Ben couldn't breathe. He lost his hold on Dan's arm and Dan instantly spun round to clasp him in a vice-like grip. Dan's eyes blazed with rage as he pressed Ben ever tighter. Ben pushed hard back at Dan's face, bending his neck until the strain made Dan's grip falter. Ben scampered away from him then sprang forward, shoulder first, with all his might. Dan caved in, flopping to the ground, and Ben delivered a series of blows to his face.

Blood started to flow from Dan's nose, and he became too dazed to fight back.

"We found proof!" Ben yelled at him, wanting to pound the truth into the boy's thick head. "Proof to show all of you! We know everything about Mothership!"

"Ben! Please stop!" Han cried, but Ben had already exhausted his anger. He knelt over Dan, gasping for breath.

"It's all your fault," Dan whimpered. It seemed as if he was going to cry. "You and Han. You're breaking Mothership. You're upsetting Jones. You're not doing what you're told. Your fault. It's all your fault."

"Well ask Jones. Ask him yourself," Ben panted.

They looked in the opened door of Jones' room and saw him slumped across the bed, his hands on the floor and his head sagging.

They rushed to him and Han propped him up. Beside him was the needle and the empty tube. His eyes were open, but his gaze was blank.

"He's dead!" Dan cried, "Jones is dead!"

CHAPTER 14

The Choice

HAN felt Jones' wrist. "He's alive," she said. Gus stared at the man's gaping face, not understanding how the hero of his stories could now be so strange.

"Then what's wrong with him?" he asked.

"I don't know. But it's nothing we can do anything about," Han said. "Now you're all coming down to the play area. There's something you're going to see whether you want to or not. It's a true story — about us."

"Luke," Ben said, taking his own gun back from Han, "get Dan's gun."

Luke giggled.

"Who — me?"

"Yes. And use it on anyone if you have to."

Luke went out and picked up the gun. He wanted to shoot Dan right there and then, but decided that it was best to wait and hope Dan would do something wrong.

"One false move, Piggie," he said, giddy with this new-found power, "and you go through the wall. Now move."

* * * *

Han put the video disc of 'Project Ark' in the TV wall player and turned to the assembled group.

"We have even more evidence if you need it, but this is the truth about Mothership and why we're here." She set the disc playing and sat back, watching the faces around her rather than the screen. Many times before they had gathered and watched old videos and cartoons. Now she wondered how they would react to these devastating facts about Earth.

As the truth was revealed, some muttered among themselves and others gazed silently. Eve clutched Jim's hand. Luke frowned, amazed by what he saw. Dan watched without emotion. He simply wiped his bloodied nose with his sleeve and gazed at the screen.

When the film showed the construction of Mothership, a gasp of recognition rose from some of the group. Anne and Con insisted at first that the dying planet shown couldn't possibly be Earth. Seeing Jones among the crew, however, confirmed to them that the ship described as UWP Ark was, indeed, Mothership. As the video disc ended, Han switched off the screen.

"The rest of the story is on the crew reports we can show to you on control deck. We've kept the link open and you can all come up with us to see for yourselves. They were nearly thirty years into the mission when Mothership was badly damaged. Four of the crew died. We twelve were born before all the seeds of life forms were lost. Then Jones' wife was killed trying to repair the damage, and Jones went mad. This ship won't get to Planet Ararat before our supplies run out. The way we're travelling now,

the journey would take three hundred years."
There was silence for a long while.
"Jones wouldn't lie to us," Gus finally said.
"It's all a trick," Anne said.
"Someone made this up," Dan concluded. Ike and Kay chimed in their agreement.
"Jones says we're going back to Earth."
Ben was amazed.
"You must believe your own eyes," he said.
"You've shown us your film," Dan was dismissive, "but what do we know about it? Or what do we know about Mothership? Do we believe this thing you found when you were out of bounds, or do we believe Jones?"
"If you need more proof we have it," Han said.
"There are plenty of things we don't know," Dan said, ignoring her, "that's the way it should be. The only person who knows everything on Mothership is Jones. And he's the only one I'd believe."
"But he admitted it to us!" Ben insisted, "that's what he was telling us before you barged in."
"Well then let him tell the rest of us. Let him tell us that Project Ark isn't a deliberate lie — a trick, maybe, to be used if someone from another planet tried to steal the treasures we're bringing back to Earth."
"Any of you who want to come with us can see the truth for themselves," Han said, "if you need to see the dead crew members, the destroyed life support area, the cargo area where Jones was living. It's all here on Mothership. All you have to do is come with us."
"It's out of bounds," Ike said, and the others murmured agreement.
"You have to break the rules," Han said, "that's the only way of finding the real truth."
"We do what Jones said." It seemed that Dan spoke for all of them.
"You found this where Jones was living?" Luke asked.
"Yes. Hidden away from us."

"Jones didn't want us to know what was going on," Luke said, "he lied to us."

"Jones wouldn't lie," Dan snapped, but Luke didn't react to the voice that he had feared for years.

"Okay, let's just imagine something," Gus said. The others listened intently to him. Being the storyteller, he was the one who had given so much detail to the version of truth they had always accepted. "Supposing something really is wrong with Mothership and right now it's damaged. Well, we're all okay aren't we? We don't see any signs of damage, do we? So it can't be that bad. And I'm sure Earth will send help to us if it's needed. We just have to wait. That's the very worst that can be going on."

Ben spoke quietly.

"Gus — we've been travelling away from Earth for forty years, and we've been out of contact with it for thirteen. We can't transmit to Earth and they can't send anything to help us. It's up to us now. We're on our own in space. You understand?"

"I say what I know," Gus replied, "Jones is the adult. We have to believe him."

"And if he tells you, as he already admitted to us, that Mothership is a failed project limping away from Earth?"

Gus thought for some moments. All watched and waited for his response.

"Then I'd think Jones wasn't well because of the accident he had when he was trying to get to Earth ahead of us."

Ben turned to Han. There was simply no winning. Han was unmoved by the reaction of the group. She had long suspected that the others were too afraid and locked into the dull life on Mothership to ever admit that something was wrong. She had often thought that she was the only one on board who was hungry for the truth. It was good at least to know that Ben was on her side. She was about to suggest that they go their own way and forget the others when Fay stood up.

She flicked dark brown hair off her forehead as she stared around at the others. She was always the quiet one, but this time she would dare to say what was on her mind.

"I believe Ben and Han," she began nervously, "and I say we should do something. Sometimes — and I don't know why — I can see things and sense things that no one else knows about. It's been happening more and more lately. I see grown-ups — more like the shadows of grown-ups. A woman comes to me in my dreams to tell me we have to do something. I'm sure that what Han and Ben say is what she's been trying to tell me."

The others looked at her dumbly, thinking only that she was strange and beyond believing.

"Fay is right. And she has the courage to believe we should do something," said Luke, and Fay flashed a smile at him. "It never seemed right to me. It never really made sense until now. We have the truth."

"Anyone else?" Ben asked, but the others remained silent.

"Well this is what I think," Han declared. "There are now two camps. Those who want to stay on Mothership doing nothing, and those who want to take action. Me, Ben, Luke and Fay are going to the control deck. We're going to study the information and make a decision. I warn the rest of you not to try stopping us."

Dan laughed.

"You're nothing but trouble," he said. "Go if you want to go. Fall into space, or get burned up, or choke or starve or anything else. We're sick of you and the trouble you make."

He went to the TV wall and stared at the blank screen.

"What have you told us? Just another story. Well I don't believe your story." He pressed the eject button on the player and the disc slid out. He held it between his blood stained fingers. "Project Ark? Who's to say when that happened. Who's to say it wasn't something else

107

Mothership did on its adventures around the universe? We don't know and we've no way of knowing. We have to believe Jones and wait until we reach Earth. Nothing else is true." He flung the disc across the room and it shattered against the wall. "You know what I think? You've found all the treasure Mothership is bringing back to Earth, and you're trying to steal it for yourself. You want to scare us off the ship, or maybe take the treasure and go to Earth on your own so you can sell the treasure and be richer than anyone else."

Luke stepped forward, staring at Dan.

"You used to call me a fool," he said, "well you're the fool. And anyone who listens to you is a fool."

"Just wait till Jones hears about this," Dan fumed helplessly, "wait till Jones wakes up and we tell him what you're doing."

"Enough," Han said. "If you don't want to see the truth, there's no point trying to convince you. The four of us have work to do. As for the rest of you — there's still time to change your minds. But I'm not expecting it. Let's go."

She slung her sound gun off her shoulder, ready to take action if anyone were so foolish as to try stopping her. Ben, Luke and Fay followed her out of the room as the others watched in silence.

The four strode up the winding corridor to the end door which Han and Ben had kept open. Ben turned to Luke and Fay as they entered the chamber. He was self-assured and spoke like an old expert.

"This chamber leads to the link between decks. When the door seals, the roof opens and we lose gravity — gravity is what keeps your feet on the ground. But don't be afraid. Me and Han will help you and it'll be okay."

Han glanced at him and smiled, remembering the first time he'd entered the link. As the roof opened and the floor began to rise, Fay and Luke joined the adventure.

CHAPTER 15

Luke and Fay

B EN was able to lead Fay and Luke through the wonderland of the control deck, showing them the computer rooms, the fusion reactor and master control. Luke was surprised to find that he understood some of the technology. The classroom lessons he'd seen while staying clear of trouble had actually rubbed off.

Fay had little understanding of the technology. Despite her sensing a truth greater than the stories she never imagined Mothership was so big and complex.

Han was busy searching through discs and files for information on the planet XT25 Jones had spoken of. It was not on any of the files for Project Ark, although she searched back through the computer memory and the graphics of this region of space. When nothing gave her the required information, she went back into history files on the space probe research for Project Ark. There, at last, she found the lead to what she was looking for — Helen Jones had created a file on the planet as part of research she had been carrying out. To her great excitement Han soon found Helen Jones' own report and assessment of the planet.

Sitting down with Ben, Luke, and Fay, she ran the file to discover just what their chances of survival might be on XT25.

* * * *

Gus didn't want to tell the story even though Dan ordered him to. No one wanted to hear it anyway. It had become too confusing to think about in the light of doubts and challenges from Han and Ben.

"Are we going to let them do this?" Dan was sour. He glared at the others as they sat in the play area. Jones still couldn't be woken, and it seemed that no one wanted to play or talk anymore. "Are we going to just let them walk through here when they come back and then leave Mothership? We don't know what they're taking. We don't know what damage they're doing. Are we just going to let them get away with it?"

"How can we stop them?" Anne asked.

"By being strong," Dan said. He clenched his red fists. "By not letting them go."

It was the first stirring of some kind of reaction in the group. They could unite against the four rebels.

"We're here to take care of Mothership — aren't we?" Dan roared. "Are we going to let them destroy what we are here to defend?"

Their excitement grew. Dan overturned a games table, kicking at its legs to break them away. He yelled to the others, his eyes wild with rage.

"They can't trick us! We don't fall for their trap! I say we fight back!"

* * * *

Helen Jones had recorded an introduction to her file. "XT25 was studied for the project because it was so much nearer to Earth than Planet Ararat. However, it offers a very hostile environment," she explained, "the planet is in the early stages of evolution. The atmosphere is only just within human tolerance, and the temperature swings between day and night are extreme. To survive on XT25, people would have to face hardships more severe than those on Earth as it has become."

The computer file ran a hologram showing Planet XT25 and pre-ice-age Earth side by side for comparison. A scroll of data beneath ran details of their suitability for habitation. The most obvious factor to consider was the fact that XT25 was half again as large as Earth, and the data showed how this would affect the human body through increased weight and effort required on the planet.

"It seems likely that there would be edible vegetation and other life forms — though there is far less likelihood of hominid life there than on Planet Ararat," Helen's voice continued, "XT25 is still at a stage which is hostile to the evolving of anything similar to the human race."

The hologram of XT25 showed its violent climate and many active volcanoes. There were vast ice regions and a rich, green equator which was draped in swirling clouds. Helen's report explained the many dangers. Space probe research had shown a high radioactive content in the atmosphere which far exceeded the safe limits for human life. There seemed to be little in favour of diverting Mothership to the planet.

"I will now begin work on a possible scenario for making life bearable on Planet XT25," Helen concluded, "I want to know if there are ways by which some corner of the grim planet could be turned into a new home for this lost caravan of humanity."

Helen had not lived even to begin that research. The group were left facing an option that seemed to offer very little hope. "It may be our only way out," Han said, "but we might never survive there."

"How would we get there in the first place?" Fay asked.

"There are emergency escape craft on the transport deck," Han explained. "They could carry the four of us and enough supplies. We're talking about a journey of almost a year. That alone will be very difficult for us, and we'll have to trust that there's food on the planet we can eat, a cave we can heat and no life forms that would see us as food. We'll be living a primitive and dangerous life. The comforts of Mothership will be a thing of the past."

"I think that since the alternative is staying on Mothership there's only one choice," Ben decided, "if we stay we live and die here for nothing. I know I don't want that."

He was all in favour of the adventure. He felt it was a chance to live in a real world with maybe real rivers to drift along.

"I want to go to XT25," Han said. "I'm sure about that. But we can't push Fay and Luke into joining us."

"I know one thing for sure," Luke said, "I don't want to stay on Mothership. Not with Dan and the others. Even if they live on and on here and we die on that planet. I don't care. I'd rather take a chance than stay here."

"All this explains something to me," Fay added, "for a long time I've had dreams of being drawn to some strange, angry place. Even though I felt cut off from the known, I was aware of adult faces smiling and saying this is the right way. I'm sure it's what we're meant to do."

The four were united, and certain of the path to follow. Ben reached out his hand to Han who, smiling, reached out a hand to clench his. Then Luke and Fay joined with their hands.

"Here's to the future," Han said.

"To the future," they declared.

* * * *

They gathered all they needed from the control deck — a computer programme for operating the escape craft, the flight plan to XT25 and a sound gun for Fay.

As they passed through the link they prepared themselves for their last descent to what they once thought of as the sum total of their world — the living deck of Mothership. They were ready with their guns in case the others tried to stop them.they came out of the link expecting trouble.

Instead, all was silent. Unusually silent. Han was suspicious.

"Let's get out of here as fast as we can," she whispered.

The four moved quickly down past the sleeping and feeding areas. As they reached the door to the play area Ike, Gus, Anne and Kay stepped out brandishing sticks.

Han, Ben, Luke and Fay stared at their opponents. Once they had all been Mothership's family.

"We have guns," Han said, "let us pass."

"No." Dan stood behind them with Jim, Eve, and Con. "You're trying to steal the treasure."

"Talk to Jones," Ben said.

"He's still the same." Dan moved closer. "And if we let you go you'll put us all in danger. So we're going to keep you here. You can stop some of us with your sound guns, but you can't stop all of us. So you're not going anywhere."

Dan rushed forward and Luke shot him. Attacked from both sides, the four shot quickly and some of the others fell back. They burst through the line and ran down the corridor firing their guns. But in the frenzy their aim was poor. Han and Luke tripped over wires that had been set as traps. As Ben went to help Han, the others were upon them. Eve struck first, hitting Luke across the head and bringing him to his knees. They swarmed into each other, the guns being the main prize for the clutching hands.

The sheer weight of bodies on them soon had the four bloodied. Ben was held by Jim and Ike as Dan beat him again and again. Han kicked out wildly but she was overpowered by Con and Anne. Dan was crazed by the fight and he was capable of killing Ben.

"Let us go! Let us go!", Fay cried out, pleading with the others.

But no one would listen. It seemed they were about to become the prisoners of Dan and his gang.

CHAPTER 16

Huck Finn

"Stop it! Stop it now!" They looked up. Jones was leaning against the wall, looking sicker than they'd ever seen him before. His face was blotchy red and white. It was hard for him even to stay on his feet, and he spoke slowly between rasping breaths.

"Let them go. Now. They have the right to do what they want to do."

He moved closer.

"But we can't," Dan protested.

"Shut up Dan. I order it," Jones sighed.

"They'll destroy Mothership!" Dan cried "They'll steal the treasure! They'll fall into the rockets! All the things you said..."

Dan rubbed his head. He was so confused he ran out of protests. Instead, he pleaded with Jones.

"What's the truth?" His voice shook. For the first time,

he was truly afraid. "Tell us. Tell me. What's the truth?"

Jones shook his head.

"You decide. You're the one who has to live by it."

Jones reached out to Han. She went hesitantly to him. A faint, desperate smile flicked across his face as he laid his hand on her shoulder.

"You," he whispered, "you remind me of Helen. You have that fire. That strength. So if you think there's a way out, take it. I can't say what will happen. I think you have little chance of survival. But go. If you need to go, go."

Jones turned to Ben.

"We're going to XT25," Ben said.

"Listen to me, boy," Jones said, "you are brave and young. You two — stay together. Some day, if you live, you'll have children. With you as their parents, they may just have the courage to make that planet their home. Maybe you're the true seed. Maybe you'll make the madness of Mothership worthwhile." Jones nodded to himself. He was racked with pain, and could feel the last of his strength fade away. He looked at the four young rebels and smiled.

"Safe journey."

Han and Ben stepped away from him. Luke and Fay gathered up the guns. The four of them walked down the winding corridor watched solemnly by the others. Han glanced back one last time at Jones. The others had gathered around him as he slumped to the ground. She felt sad for them all.

As they passed the schoolrooms Luke halted.

"Wait," he said, "I'm forgetting something."

He went into a classroom and searched under the chairs for his schoolwork computer.

"I'd been writing things in this about Mothership, and I'm going to keep it with me. I'm going to write the story of our adventure for other people to read some day."

Then Ben realised he had left behind his own prize possession — his book. It was too late to turn back. He would have to leave without 'The Adventures of Huckleberry Finn'.

"You do that," Ben smiled, "you write something better than Huckleberry Finn."

The four entered the link at the end door and travelled on through the life support deck. Fay and Luke were stunned by the discovery of the place where they were born. Arriving in cargo deck, they set about preparing for the voyage ahead.

* * * *

It took three days' work to make the emergency escape craft ready. It was designed for fifty passengers, and they removed the extra seats to create space for supplies and room to sleep. Ben, Luke and Fay gathered food, tools and medicine from the cargo deck to store on board. Han set to work learning to programme and control the ship.

The voyage would last ten months by her reckoning. They would not be very comfortable on the trip, but the journey ahead would be tolerable and they could cope.

When Han had completed her work she set about doing what Helen Jones had planned to do — launching a pod into space heading towards Earth transmitting an SOS emergency signal from the crippled Mothership. Han felt that the signal pod was as much a simple tribute to Helen Jones as a message for Planet Earth. She gave a private salute to Helen's memory as the pod spun away into space.

Finally all work was completed and the four were ready to begin their voyage. They ran a last checklist of details, then all stood together in the craft thinking about what lay ahead. Luke was very sullen.

"I must be a real coward," he said, "I feel so scared."

Ben put an arm around him.

"We live our own lives now, Luke," he said, "Jones or Dan won't be around anymore trying to bully us into lying about what's happening or how we feel. We're all scared and that's okay."

"Jones wanted us to hide from the truth and from ourselves," Han added, "but we won't do that anymore. We're free to be ourselves."

Luke smiled and sobbed at the same time, and this made him laugh at himself.

"Yeah," he chuckled, "we're free."

"You know," Fay said, "it seems odd to be setting off on this craft without having a name for it."

"A name?" The thought hadn't occurred to Han.

"I have a name for it," Ben said, "if you'll agree, I'd like us to call it the Huck Finn."

"The Huck Finn," Luke repeated, liking the sound of the words. "I'd go along with that."

"The Huck Finn it is then," the others agreed.

When the time for departure came, Han and Ben sat at the controls in the cockpit. Luke and Fay were behind them watching in fear and anticipation.

As Han began the countdown to igniting the engines, Ben triggered the opening of the huge exit. As its iris opened, stars stretched out before them. The sight was breathtaking — their only previous view of the stars had been through the portholes on Mothership. Now space was ahead ready to embrace them in all its vastness.

The craft rose and made its first gentle move into freedom. The four friends smiled, not knowing what lay in store, but knowing that the future beckoned and it was their destiny to embark on this adventure. The Huck Finn glided out into space. Their hearts pounded with fear as the break was made — behind them, the iris closed on the world of Mothership forever. It was no longer their world and never would be again.

"What do you think will happen to Mothership?" Luke asked.

"Who knows," Han replied. "I think Jones is dying. But I don't think that he matters anymore. They believe what they want to believe and they'll go on that way no matter what."

"Maybe they'll go on that way to their death," Fay said, "fooling themselves with the stories."

The craft drew away from Mothership, and as it did they could see the gash across the life support deck. The pod that Helen had piloted was still there, like a sentry, at the mouth of the gap. Sparks still flashed from the depths of Mothership's wound.

Han fired the main thrusters of the Huck Finn. As they moved further away they could see Mothership in all its majesty — a great tower of metal, limping through space. In spite of her searches inside it, Han had never appreciated just how huge the ship was.

"The biggest, the bravest" she mumbled to herself, thinking of Jones' wild rantings.

But as time went by, a strange thing happened. As they travelled further and further away from that vast tower of human achievement, its importance also seemed to disappear into starry space. Indeed, they hardly noted the day when they couldn't identify Mothership amidst the shimmer of the stars.

*   *   *   *

Long into the journey, Ben had a dream. He dreamt he was visiting Mothership after many years. Children ran around the living deck scrambling among adults he didn't recognise. He walked on, into the play area which was shabby — all its seats torn or broken.

In the corner was an ancient man surrounded by a group of squealing children.

"Tell it! Tell it!" they were pleading. "Tell the story Uncle Gus! Please tell it!"

The old man smiled, his face wrinkling with deep cracks of age across his cheeks and forehead.

"Once upon a time a long time ago," he began, "there were eight space travellers who went on a great adventure across the universe. They travelled to new planets and made friends there and gathered all kinds of knowledge and wealth...."

Ben opened his eyes. In the tapestry of space before him he could identify a glowing object that had a texture to it — not the constant glare of a star. It was a planet. He checked the chart of the flight path and fixed the position of this new object. He smiled as he nudged Han awake.

"XT25," he whispered, and she looked out.

"Yes," she said, "it's time to start our preparations."

Han woke Luke and Fay to show them the planet and discuss the procedures for orbiting and landing. But Ben wasn't listening. He was thinking of a river, and a clay pipe, and the glory of real adventures in a real world. He whispered a word as he looked at the planet. One simple, magical word:

"Home."

— THE END —